The **Viagra** Diaries

"A smart, witty, sometimes hilarious coming-of-age novel for and about the boomer generation . . . This realistic and funny novel will appeal to women of all ages, while men should find it attractively controversial."

—*Kirkus*

"A funny, poignant picture of dating, romantic love, parenting an adult daughter, and sex after sixty . . . Barbara Rose Brooker tells the truth!"

—Joan Rivers

"Barbara Rose Brooker is fearless. *The Viagra Diaries* does for single seniors what Helen Gurley Brown's *Sex and the Single Girl* and Erica Jong's *Fear of Flying* did for the women's sexual revolution in the sixties and seventies. Through the eyes of the wonderfully witty, wounded, and wistfully romantic Anny Applebaum, we discover a world few authors have dared to enter—the dating lives of the over-sixty set. What we find there is humor, heartache, and hope."

—Bradly Bessey, co-executive producer, *Entertainment Tonight*

"I love this book! I love that Anny Applebaum defies the fallacy of age. I laughed out loud at the irreverent humor and wit. But most of all, I love Anny's struggle to find herself and her essence and the fabulous love affair she has with Marv Rothstein. Through it all she discovers she can have it all: Love, laughs, fame, fortune and sex. Thank you, Barbara, for giving women another example of what's possible."

—Sally Kellerman, actor and singer

"I raced through Barbara Rose Brooker's moral tale of a seventy-year-old pilgrim fighting for her life. Her hero (I mean Anny) wants both: love (and not just sex) and art. I laughed out loud at her trials, for Brooker's story is moral and satiric, political and comic. At times I thought of Chaucer and always I applauded Brooker's perfect ear for the speech of old men and ingénues, her poetic language and her guts."

—Phyllis Koestenbaum, author of
Doris Day and Kitschy Melodies: Prose Poems

THE
Viagra
Diaries

BARBARA ROSE BROOKER

GALLERY BOOKS

New York   London   Toronto   Sydney   New Delhi

Gallery Books
A Division of Simon & Schuster, Inc.
1230 Avenue of the Americas
New York, NY 10020

This book is a work of fiction. Names, characters, places, and incidents either are products of the author's imagination or are used fictitiously. Any resemblance to actual events or locales or persons, living or dead, is entirely coincidental.

Copyright © 2013 by Barbara Brooker

All rights reserved, including the right to reproduce this book or portions thereof in any form whatsoever. For information address Gallery Books Subsidiary Rights Department, 1230 Avenue of the Americas, New York, NY 10020.

First Gallery Books trade paperback edition April 2013

GALLERY BOOKS and colophon are registered trademarks of Simon & Schuster, Inc.

For information about special discounts for bulk purchases, please contact Simon & Schuster Special Sales at 1-866-506-1949 or business@simonandschuster.com.

The Simon & Schuster Speakers Bureau can bring authors to your live event. For more information or to book an event contact the Simon & Schuster Speakers Bureau at 1-866-248-3049 or visit our website at www.simonspeakers.com.

Designed by Jaime Putorti

Manufactured in the United States of America

10 9 8 7 6 5 4 3 2 1

Library of Congress Cataloging-in-Publication Data is available.

ISBN 978-1-4516-8861-0
ISBN 978-1-4516-8862-7 (ebook)

I dedicate this book and all my love to my daughters,

Suzy Unger and Bonny Lisa Osterman.

To Emilia Pisani, my smart editor, who made this book possible,

and David Vigliano, the best agent.

My deepest appreciation to my students,

who are tomorrow's authors.

THE
Viagra
Diaries

Chapter 1

Van Gogh's *Starry Night* blows my mind. God, it's something, swirling stars, wild emotions, and vibrant colors. Wow, there's nothing like art.

Anyway, my name is Anny Applebaum. I'm sixty-five and I write a seniors' lifestyle column for the *San Francisco Times*. I'm at the San Francisco Museum of Contemporary Art, taking notes for my next column. I usually write about restaurants, gyms, social events, stuff like that, but I'm hoping a column about art will be more inspiring.

It's getting late, so I hurry down the flight of stairs, into the huge marble lobby with all these terrific Calders swinging around, and rush outside. It's raining like crazy and I lost my umbrella so I make a run for it, careful not to fall in my four-inch, leather, high-heel boots. It's rush hour and people are

1

opening umbrellas, hurrying onto streetcars. God, the city is beautiful, all these hills surrounding the bay. A native, I never get tired of the city. It's like living inside one of those little glass balls you shake up.

By now I'm soaked, walking along the sides of the buildings to Union Square, thinking I'll get the next bus home, but the rain is harder and lightning streaks the sky. I hurry into a café, deciding to stay there until the storm stops.

The café is small and cozy. A few people sit at tables, working on their laptops. I take off my coat and fedora, shaking out the rain, and sit next to the window. I order a cup of coffee, thinking I'll take notes for tomorrow's column, but my cell phone rings. It's my editor, Monica. I've been a columnist at the paper for five years and she rarely calls, so I know something must be up. "Hello," I exuberantly say.

"Bad news," Monica says quickly, before I get a word in. She's on speakerphone, and I can picture her smoking a cigarette. "Sales are down big-time at the paper."

"Tomorrow's column is going to be great," I quickly say in my most assuring tone. "I'm writing about van Gogh and that the museum is a place for seniors to—"

"Anny, our seniors are in diapers. They don't know from van Gogh. There's no market for seniors. Unless you find some new angle, some controversy, I have to cut the column," Monica says in her fast voice.

"Seniors write me that they're tired of ageism and being

put into an age category. Stuff like that," I say, trying not to sound upset.

"Unless the *San Francisco Times* is making money, fans mean nothing," Monica snaps. "Nada. I can't run 'Seniors and Politics.' You mostly talk about your antiwar views and how the world is messed up."

"I only said that I thought the Iraq war was a waste, and that seniors should protest and get involved."

"You're not Christiane Amanpour. If we wanted a political commentator, we'd hire one. I warned you to tone down your opinions. You accused the Happy Convalescent Home of terrible conditions! I've received calls from the owner of the paper. And she's a moron."

I bite my tongue, fighting the urge to tell Monica that I'm a senior too and that I don't like the way she's talking about seniors but warning myself not to burn bridges. "I hate the label *senior*. I hate all labels: *gay, straight, senior citizen*." I argue in my nicest tone. "I'm sixty-five, but I'm not a senior. I'm a person. As soon as you're fifty, if you don't like look like one of those drippy housewives of Orange County, you're relegated to assisted living. I'd like to write about ageism. That's controversial."

"Hey, girl. No one wants to read about getting old. Nor do our readers want to read about seniors acting like John Travolta in *Saturday Night Fever*. Most of our seniors are in wheelchairs, recovering from strokes. If you don't come up with something hot, and controversial, I have to let you go."

"Sure. No offense, Monica, but you're thirty-eight and you don't suffer from age discrimination. Anyway, I'll come up with something."

"Hey, Anny. I believe in you. We've worked together going on six years. I like you, but I'm taking orders from Bunny Silverman, who thinks this is the *New York Times*. So come up with something that evokes a huge response. Gotta go."

After I hang up I feel panicked, my body shaking. I wish I had my paper bag. When I'm nervous I blow into a paper bag. I hold a paper napkin over my mouth, breathing deeply. *Please, God, I can't lose my column. I need the money.* As it is, even with Medicare and Social Security, and occasionally selling my paintings, I can hardly make it. Here I am a sixty-five-year-old, divorced columnist with no money, and sleeping on a sofa bed. But I want fame, fortune, and undying love. I want it all. And I'm sick of everyone saying I'm too old. Age has nothing to do with dreams.

As long as I can remember, I've wanted to be a writer, even imagined myself a famous journalist like Diane Sawyer, standing in the rain in some Godforsaken country, my hair soaked, while the world is crashing behind me, and then rushing to the office to write about it. Sometimes it's hard to face that so much time has passed and nothing significant has happened.

I order more coffee and watch the cable cars chugging along the hill, remembering the years I spent writing a novel, which I shelved after my marriage, then in my thirties going to graduate school and finishing my master's in creative writing. Then after my divorce, writing columns for throwaway papers, about socialites, restaurant reviews, real estate. Things were terrible until five years ago, when I pitched Monica— barged into her office, with lists of ideas about seniors, until she said, "Cool it. You're hired. I like your ideas."

I watch the rain slide along the windows, remembering the day Donald told me he wanted a divorce. I had found Viagra in Donald's suit pocket, and when I confronted him about it, he admitted he was having sex with Conchita, our twenty-year-old housekeeper, and demanded a divorce. Then to top it off, he declared bankruptcy, pleading poverty. I got a small settlement and moved to my current apartment in San Francisco. Right after the divorce, he married Conchita and they had two sons. Talk about devastated. And he has yet to contact our daughter, Emily, who at forty-one still waits for his calls. It's pathetic. I feel bad for Emily. Donald and I weren't attentive parents. I was always painting or writing and dreaming of a career. Donald was busy with his law practice and buying properties, and early on Emily was forced into the caregiver role.

It stops raining. I pay my bill, wanting to catch the six-thirty bus home, thinking that later tonight I'll work on my boxes. I make and paint boxes. I have this thing about boxes. I collect them from construction sites, and in them I create little worlds, tiny tableaux that inspire my paintings. But lately I've been in a rut and my work feels dull.

I button my black leather coat and hurry outside, running up the hill to Sutter Street, where I catch my bus.

I push myself onto the crowded bus, trying to grab a seat in the front.

"Hey, old lady. Take it easy," says a pimple-faced boy wearing a smelly parka, taking the seat. I pause for a moment, taken aback, before pushing to the back of the bus and finally getting a seat next to the window.

As the bus rattles slowly along the hills, passing rows of candy-colored Victorian houses, I catch my reflection in the window, wondering if I look old. There are circles under my eyes and my brown hair hangs limp to my shoulders. Hardly like those girls on shampoo ads, their hair so silky it floats. What *is* old, anyway? In this country, anything over twenty is old. I close my eyes, remembering last week at Emily's house. She lives in Berkeley with her partner, Harry, a fifty-year-old architect, and their black Lab, Fred. They were urging me to go on JDate, insisting that it was time I met someone. "Before you get too old, Mom, and end up in a nursing home," Emily said. But I had protested, saying that I didn't want to meet anyone online. Emily is always worrying about me, telling me what to do. It drives me crazy.

Since the divorce, outside of seeing my best friends, Janet and Lisa—we talk every night on the phone and tell each other everything—and my neighbor Ryan McNally, I don't go out much. Ryan is ten years younger, and an award-winning photographer for *National Geographic*. He lives in my building, and nine years ago we met in the laundry room. I had just moved in, and we were waiting for the dryers to finish our wash. We started talking and I found myself telling him about my recent divorce. He confided that he was a widower. We became friends, and when he's not traveling on assignment, we go to films, museums, art openings, and often critique each other's work. He knows a lot about art, and we both love art. On weekends he stays at his country house in Sebastopol, where he grows flowers.

The bus stops at Broadway and I get off. Dark now, the moon is starting to spread in the sky. I walk the two blocks to my apartment, pause by the roses in front, remembering that two months ago before Ryan left for Holland, he cut pink roses and instructed me how to cut the stems underwater before I put them in a vase.

I rush into the Moorish lobby, past the fake waterfall, and up the crooked, bumpy flight of steps to my apartment, inhaling the sweet aromas of Persian cooking and Chinese takeout floating along the hallways. I pass the empty apartment across the hall from mine, thinking that I don't want to die alone on my sofa bed like poor Mrs. Nelson, who was carried out in a body bag and with everyone looking.

I open my door, glad to face the night.

Chapter 2

N ear midnight, and I can't sleep. After my motley dinner of sardines and crackers, and watching the lousy news on CNN, I change into paint-splattered jeans and a work shirt. I tie my hair into a ponytail and turn up the salsa music. I can't work without music. I prepare my palette and lay out my tools.

I begin working on *Romance Boxes*, a set of Lucite shoeboxes I found in Chinatown and filled with poems and rose petals. Large canvases that Ryan had helped me stretch lean along the walls. Then there are the *Hanging Boxes*, rubber boxes I found in a magic store, dangling from narrow, looped cords. Painting excites me. The images help me see my reality, clarify what I don't know or can't say. It's an amazing process. I've had a dealer for several years, and though I don't think of my painting as a source of income, I do fantasize about someday having a solo show of my work.

Though my apartment is small, the eighteen-foot ceilings give it an illusion of space. French doors separate the living area from the tiny Pullman kitchen and a dining area, which I've converted into my studio. Years ago, Ryan helped build bookshelves for my books, paints, and canvases. Colorful Mexican vases from the Marin flea market are filled with orange tea roses. No matter how broke I am, every week I go to the Flower Mart and buy tea roses. Framed photographs of Emily are on a long, white table against the wall, along with photographs of Ryan and other friends.

I drill tiny holes inside the boxes, then insert tiny lights, highlighting the glass cubes on the bottom. Next, I work on *Wedding Box*, a square, papier-mâché box with holes punched on top. I want the box to reflect virginal love. I dip a brush into white acrylic paint mixed with dried flowers and apply the paint until it glows. For the next hour, I glue loose pearls into the holes.

Exhausted now, I stop working. The room is cold and I close the windows. The rain is coming in fast torrents. Pretty yellow leaves stick to the windows like damp stars; traffic swishes through the cold, drenched streets.

Wanting to clean up before I go to bed, I wash my brushes, letting them dry in coffee cans, and then I drop the tubes of paints into the large plastic bin I keep under my desk. Finally, I place the piles of *New Yorker* magazines and the *New York*

Times into the wicker trunk, trying to keep a semblance of order in my cluttered apartment. I love chaos; it's a way of keeping order. I have slight dyslexia, so my words go backward. But I have my own order and color-code my brushes, canvas, and other things. Chaos inspires me. Too much order stifles me.

Stretching my arms, I glance at a colorful photograph of Ryan I took a few months ago, before he left for Holland. He's pruning roses. His muscular, fit body bends over the roses, sunlight lighting his gold, gray-speckled, curly hair. Next to it is a photograph of Emily and Fred.

Except for the slow sound of the receding traffic outside and an occasional shrill siren, the old apartment building is quiet, and suddenly I feel alone, so alone, wondering, is this how it's going to be for the rest of my life? Sometimes I have nightmares that I'll have a stroke and Emily will have me carted to a convalescent home and I'll be sitting in a deck chair in the hallway with dirty hair and thick glasses, drooling, a Velcro name tag pinned to my floral robe from Costco. Shivering, I put the old, red shawl Emily made me years ago over my shoulders, thinking that maybe Emily and Harry are right—that I should go on JDate. Though Emily is often bossy, more the mother than the child, she is often right. We worry about each other.

Anyway, what's the big deal? Everyone is online. So why not go on JDate? Who would know, anyway?

At this thought, with new energy, I hurry to my desk.

On my laptop, I go on to JDate, register, make a payment for only three months, following the directions. I type in my screen name: *LadyAnny*. After I fill out a questionnaire stating that I prefer men from fifty-five to ninety and that I'm not interested in marriage, don't smoke, and am a liberal, I write my ad:

Sixty-five-year-old columnist seeks fun and romance with a man who is educated, has humor, and is not afraid of the rain. Be brave. Age doesn't matter. Contact me. Finally, I upload the latest photo that is used on my column.

After receiving an e-mail saying I'm an official member of JDate, exhilarated by this new experience, I spend the next hour scrolling through photographs, surprised by the vast number of boomer-plus men. Only, most of them request women "not a day over forty, a size six, fit, and having her own money." I laugh aloud at their screen names—SlickDick, Able Abe, Hung Harry—and look at photographs of astronauts, chefs, men on fishing boats holding huge fish they've caught; others on the golf course or standing next to airplanes. They have comb-overs, some wearing shorts, tuxedos, all citing their credentials: MDs, lawyers, billionaires, investment bankers.

I click on profiles for a sixty-six-year-old widower and boat designer; a therapist who wrote a book entitled *Happy Women*; and a handsome man, tall, slender, wearing ski clothes, standing on top of a mountain as if he owns it. His screen name is Great Guy. His profile says that he's seventy years old, a successful diamond dealer, and wants a romantic *long-term* relationship with a *mature* woman who is intelligent and independent. I like that he says *mature* woman. I e-mail that I'd like to meet him.

The next morning, at my computer, eager to check JDate, I log in, check my e-mails, and am amazed to see that so far the diamond dealer has responded. Great Guy writes:

Dear Anny. My name is Marv Rothstein. I'd like to meet you Friday evening, six thirty p.m., at Harris' cocktail lounge for dinner and drinks. E-mail back and please confirm. I'll be wearing a dark suit and I'll find you.

Impressed by his quick response, I Google him and am surprised to see that he is a world-renowned diamond dealer and has offices in South Africa, Belgium, and France. His clients are everyone from movie stars and other celebrities to political figures. Why is he on JDate? I wonder. But he's worth a date, I tell myself.

I write, *My name is Anny Applebaum. I'll see you at six thirty. I'll be wearing black. I have long, streaked dark hair, and I'm tall. Look forward to meeting you. Anny.*

Chapter 3

The next day at noon, I'm at Macy's basement café with Janet and Lisa. The huge cafeteria-style room smells of enchiladas, and shoppers stand in long lines, ordering lunch. Janet is on her lunch hour and Lisa is between showing properties.

"The boomer oldies are a nightmare," Janet says, eating a turkey sandwich. "Either they're dragging around pictures of their dead wives in bikinis, or they're so cheap they make you walk ten miles to park their cars."

Janet wears a dark blue Chanel uniform. Her hair, which had once been very red, is dyed bright orange now and piled high on top of her head. She has one of those imperfect faces that are beautiful—a prominent nose, piercing dark eyes, and red, full lips.

"You're a survivor, Anny," Lisa says. "You'll find an idea for your column." A size two, Lisa is petite, with blunt-cut, blond hair and dark, intelligent eyes. A blue Hermès scarf is draped over the shoulders of her gray Armani suit. Her turquoise Birkin bag is next to her.

Divorced for thirty years, Janet is the head buyer for Chanel at Macy's. We met nine years ago when I bought a Chanel lipstick and discovered that we have daughters the same age, that our husbands left us, and we became close friends. She had grown up in an orphanage and has since been on her own. Then I met Lisa Berman at a museum-docent luncheon, and we bonded over de Kooning and Picasso. She's sixty-two, a widow, and a highly successful commercial real estate developer. She also has a married son and a grandson, and her husband died of a heart attack ten years ago. "Anyway, I was up most of the night, browsing JDate.com," I announce, watching their faces for a reaction. "I have a date Friday night. We're meeting at Harris' for drinks and dinner. He's seventy, a wealthy diamond dealer."

"Hey! Honey! Not too shabby!" Janet says exuberantly. "The boomer-plus men I meet take me to the Olive Garden. Half of them are wearing diapers. If they cough, they fart. If they walk fast, they pee in their pants. Half the boomers are on Viagra, walking around with hard-ons, eating ExtenZe like candy and growing their pee-pees like trees."

Lisa says, "Just be careful. He could be a serial killer." She takes delicate bites from her organic-beet salad.

"Jewish men aren't serial killers," Janet snaps. "They're lawyers, doctors—"

"And Indian givers," Lisa says, then sips iced tea. "Remember the CEO I met on JDate? Veneers, a driver, penthouse? He gave me a gold Rolex watch for my birthday. As soon as I wouldn't have sex with him, he took the watch back. His dead wife's watch. A shame, because we had chemistry."

"Chemistry, *schmemistry*," Janet says, popping french fries into her mouth. "I don't want them unless they're sports. I went out with this wealthy furrier. He lives like King Tut at the Royal Towers, but he's cheap. He uses his two-for-one card, sneaks it to the waiter, like I wouldn't know."

"Janet, I don't really care if he has money—"

"Maybe he'll be the one," Janet interrupts, with a smirk. "We need to marry before you're on antidepressants, have hip replacements, and find yourself on a singles AARP cruise to Alaska. Marry him before your big whoopee is the kids coming over on a Sunday with *shmatte* flowers from Costco."

"I've had it with the marriage," I say. "I'm not sure it's possible to live with one man for the rest of your life. We're not in the Jane Austen age. We have choices."

"Choices to either be alone or with the boomer guys loaded up on Viagra," Janet says.

"Amen," Lisa agrees. She glances around the room and whispers, "And Janet's not kidding about the Viagra. It's a Viagra generation out there."

Janet makes a face. "Even the pathetic guys can do it. I was with this sixty-eight-year-old insurance tycoon, half-dead. All I did was touch one pathetic ball the size of a marble and he got off like a moose in heat. Myrna Goldblatt was on a *schlep-dick* cruise with this rich guy, and he was so loaded on Viagra that his thingy got stuck in her and she had to call the captain to call a doctor to pull them apart, like dogs."

"Oh my God," I say, trying not to laugh. "Poor thing."

"Janet!" Lisa scolds.

"Lighten up, honey," Janet says. She pauses, her soulful, dark eyes staring at my face. "You need a makeover, Anny."

Lisa nods in agreement. "You're tall, slim, but you need Botox. Your clothes are too posthippie. Get rid of the gray and put in more gold streaks. Let Hasid, my hairstylist, do it. I'll make the call."

"Give me a break! I've been in therapy for nine years, and I finally like the way I look."

They sigh, frustrated expressions on their faces. But Janet insists that I let her do a makeover. "You'll see. I'll teach you so you'll be glam for the date."

Lisa has to get back to work, and I'm asking myself, what do I have to lose? I follow Janet upstairs to the main floor.

Macy's is a zoo. Rock music blasts from speakers. At the Chanel counter in the middle of the main floor, I sit on a tall wooden stool in front of a mirror while Janet's assistant, Manuel, cleans my face with cotton balls soaked in this smelly astringent. Manuel is pipe thin, about nineteen, with spiked hair and arrogant dot eyes. He wears all black and moves as if he's dancing.

"Do you have a good cleanser?" he asks in a thick Spanish accent.

"Nivea," I meekly say.

"Very bad," Manuel says, looking alarmed. "Clogs the pores. That's why your skin looks drab. You need to exfoliate." His two assistants, who look no more than twelve, nod eagerly like a Greek chorus. By now a small crowd of shoppers encircle the chair, watching.

Janet takes over. She stands on a step stool. "Now, honey, first, we're going to apply moisturizer. Look at these lines," she says, tch-tch-tching. "When men meet me, they think I'm thirty. Look at my skin. It's smooth. Moist." She lowers her voice. "And at night I swathe my face and my you-know-what with virgin olive oil. Our you-know-whats get dry."

"Moist," I repeat.

"Close your eyes, honey," Janet says, her cigarette breathe blowing on my face. "I'm now applying cover-up on your face, covering those dark spots and tiny red veins. Nasty. Honey, this is important."

"Sure."

Next, Janet lines my eyes, then applies gray eye shadow along my eyelids, murmuring, "Smoky and sexy," lecturing that it's "key" to use blush.

"Sure. I will."

"Honey, act indifferent," she whispers, her cigarette breath in my face. "These boomer men love bitches. It turns them on. And don't put out on the first date. Let them think your you-know-what is gold."

"I'm only going on a date," I protest, embarrassed about the crowd moving closer to the chair.

"Even though my thingy is shriveled up and I dye the white hairs," she whispers, "I let them think they're not good enough to go down there."

Everyone is listening. I blush, wanting to shrink into a dot, hoping that the layers of concealer cover up my embarrassment.

Janet finishes the makeup and holds up a mirror for me to see my new look. I really like it. "It's beautiful. Thank you."

She hugs me. "Honey, romance is just around the corner. Be light. Be beautiful. Exfoliate. Drink water."

"Sure."

"Practice orgasmic sounds. They love to have you sound like a bull in heat."

Everyone is looking at my face, and listening to Janet. I feel myself blush, wondering if it shows through the bronzer.

Manuel gushes how "gorgeous" I look. "When you came in, you looked *nebbish*. Now you look like a diva."

Janet drops a handful of Chanel samples into my tote bag. We hug one more time and I rush outside to the darkening day and grab a taxi home, my head swirling with Janet's and Lisa's advice and wondering about this brave new world I'm going into.

Chapter 4

t's Friday, and I'm a wreck. In two hours I'm meeting Marv Rothstein. I can't believe I'm actually going out on a date. I feel shivers of anticipation; I haven't had a date since my divorce, and I haven't felt so nervous, so giddy, since I met my ex.

I blow-dry my hair. It's still brown, but yesterday I had gold highlights put in to blend with the gray. Emily is always harping that I'm too old to wear long hair, but I love it. The older I get, the longer it gets.

I smooth the black fishnet stockings over my legs and slip into the Joan Crawford–style platform shoes. They're black, with thin ankle straps—perfect with the black skirt covering my knees.

Carefully, I line my lips with a red pencil and then fill in with the Chanel gloss. A little Vaseline on my still-dark and thick eyebrows, then last, I spray a mist of Chanel perfume, spinning twice in it. Finally, I add my shoulder-length silver earrings, my Tibetan silver collar, and my amber rings. I love silver craft jewelry; I buy it at craft fairs.

I'm ready. I button the long, fitted, black jacket, smoothing it over my hips, turning one more time in the mirror. My cell phone rings, and I quickly answer it, thinking that it might be Marv.

"What time is he picking you up?" Emily demands. I hear breathing from the other extension.

"I'm meeting him at Harris' in the cocktail lounge."

"Let the man pick you up!" she shouts.

"I agree," says Harry on the other phone. Harry works at home. He always listens in on Emily's phone conversations. But I like him.

"So what do you know about this guy?" Emily asks in a demanding tone.

"He's seventy, divorced twice, a successful diamond dealer, world traveler. He has a son about your age, divorced twice. His picture is nice. He looks quite fit."

"How long divorced from the second wife?" Harry asks.

"I don't know yet."

"Well, be sure to ask," Emily advises. "You have to be careful, Mom."

"Love isn't a résumé," I say.

"Mom! You sound like a Hallmark greeting card," Emily

groans. "And don't talk about your divorce. Men hate that. Let him do the talking."

"I agree," Harry says.

"And make sure you play your cards right," Emily continues. "If he asks you out again, be unavailable."

"But I am available!"

"Then don't ask us! We're busy people! You don't listen!"

"Emily is just worried about you," Harry says in a sympathetic tone. "We want you to be happy."

"Bring condoms," Emily advises.

"What? I'm not having sex with a man on the first date. I'm not interested in that."

They sigh, and I hear whispering.

"What are you wearing?" Emily wants to know. "I hope not those freaky Joan Crawford thrift-store shoes. Harry agrees."

"I didn't say that," Harry says.

"I like what I'm wearing," I protest.

"Call me first thing in the morning," Emily says.

After I hang up, at my computer I read Marv Rothstein's JDate profile one more time. He majored in business at Toledo State College. He opened diamond stores and slowly built a diamond empire. I read, *I love being a grandfather. I love my six-year-old granddaughter. I love jazz and contemporary art and to tango.*

I close the computer wondering why an attractive, successful man would be on JDate. I grab my bag and step out into the hallway, thinking it's time to find out.

. . .

It's a cold January night; the moon is bright yellow, and the fog blows like silk. San Francisco is quiet except for the foghorns and the rustle of the wind. The restaurant is walking distance from my apartment, so I walk along Van Ness Avenue, avoiding the potholes, telling myself not to fall. All I need is a broken hip before my first date in decades. I hear music in my head, sensual music, and my skin is prickling with anticipation.

I arrive at the restaurant, butterflies in my stomach, and go inside.

Chapter 5

I stand inside the doorway, blinking. I have a depth-perception problem, so I take a second to get my bearings. I make my way into the cocktail lounge and sit in the corner facing the door. The place is really nice—one of those swank bars where the bartenders wear bow ties and use cocktail shakers to shake up the drinks and a combo plays "Autumn Leaves."

I'm fifteen minutes early, so I order my favorite drink: Stoli over ice with three green olives. Now I'm feeling a glow—my debts and career worries off my mind for the first time all week.

At six thirty on the dot, a tall, slender man with slicked-back, silky, silver hair accentuating a Roman nose and a moody but handsome face approaches me. He walks as if he owns the room—this aura, this arrogance, on his fixed smile, quick glance. He's elegantly dressed in a dark pinstripe suit, pale blue shirt, and burgundy silk tie. God, he's something. Really stunning. Immediately, I'm attracted.

"Anny?"

"Marv, hello." I extend my hand, thinking he's more handsome than his picture—a cross between a Jewish Clint Eastwood and Harrison Ford.

"I ordered a drink," I nervously say.

"I'll join you." His dark eyes check me out in one glance as he sits at the table.

He impatiently glances toward the waiter hovering nearby, summoning him, and orders a Cutty Sark over. "You're prettier than your picture," he says, intently looking at me as if appraising a diamond.

"You too," I say, sounding like a sap. But I can't help it. I'm totally bowled over. But his way of looking at me makes me nervous, as if he can see into me.

When his drink comes, he clicks his glass on mine. "To tonight," he says in this smooth voice. When he smiles, his teeth don't show, and his long mouth goes up in a single line. I gulp the vodka, feeling light-headed. "So tell me about your diamond business. It sounds so interesting."

In a low, modulated voice, articulate and self-assured, he tells me that he worked himself up the ladder, sells diamonds all over the world. He spends time in Zimbabwe and at his offices in Belgium and France, loves his work, and is always looking for a more perfect diamond. "Nothing is more beautiful than a perfect diamond." A wistful expression is on his face.

"Blood diamonds?" I carefully ask.

He shakes his head. "I buy diamonds at auctions or by referral. My clients range from sultans to models to movie stars. People who love beauty, and who have the money to buy true beauty." He sips his drink, gracefully holding the glass between two large fingers. "Diamonds bring me to high places. I meet beautiful people," he says wistfully.

As he continues to talk about diamonds, his travels, and aspirations to buy diamond mines, I'm thinking that everything about him arouses me: just the sound of his voice, the perfect knot in his tie, the way he holds himself so straight, as if he's looking out at the world—his swagger, his elegance, his scent of a fine subtle cologne. He's ten feet off the ground.

"So are diamonds really a girl's best friend?" I ask, my voice dropping, aware that I'm flirting.

"They are for most women," he says with a flirtatious grin.

"Guess you think my craft jewelry is corny," I say, my bracelets clinking up my arm.

"It suits you. You're arty." He pauses, barely blinking his appraising eyes. "Do you like sports?"

"I hate sports."

"I love all sports," he says, grinning. "I ski all over the world. My first wife, Gisele, was a champion French skier. She ran off with her trainer and died in a ski accident."

"I'm sorry."

"You look good for sixty-five," he says after a tense silence. "I've never dated a woman your age."

"Whoop-de-do. Haven't you heard? Sixty-five is the new forty."

"I find you very attractive. You're different."

"Do you think so?" I ask.

"I know so."

"Why did you answer my ad?" I ask, after a long moment.

He smiles and his expression changes from fun flirting to tense reflection. "I thought you sounded interesting. I saw on Google that you write a column, and I admire women who have careers." He pauses, looking intently at me. "My second ex-wife doesn't do anything except play tennis with her diamonds on and take her dog for a walk. She lives in Marin, in a fabulous home that I pay for." He pauses, and I see loneliness in his eyes, a hurt. "Anyway, we're friends."

"Uh-huh," I murmur, thinking that he might be one of those I-love-my-ex-wife freaks. He opens the menu. Carefully, he orders dinner, making sure of what I want.

By now we're easily talking. I tell him that I was married for thirty years and that I've been divorced for ten years, and about my daughter, Emily—that she lives in Berkeley with her partner, Harry, has a baking business, and that neither has been married. He has this way of listening but not commenting, as if sorting out what he wants to talk about. Then he talks about his son, a light in his shrewd eyes, especially when he talks about his granddaughter. "She's a little lady.

Adorable." For a second he looks far away, lost in reflection. "So why are you on JDate?"

I hesitate. "Like everyone else—to find love."

"Love? What is love?"

"You sound like Prince Charles. I could ask why is a man like you on JDate when you obviously meet so many people?"

He looks reflective. "I like adventure. To find that next perfect diamond."

"Anyway, I believe in love." I know that I'm giving a lot away, but wanting him to know how I feel.

He touches the side of my face, looking suddenly wistful. "Anny—you make me think of valentines, martinis on a rainy afternoon, and kisses under the stars. You're a romantic. I'll call you Valentine."

Our dinner is served. We eat poached salmon and string beans thin as threads. He picks at his food, pushing most of it to the side, while I'm starving and trying not to gulp it all. He eats neatly, slowly, his table manners impeccable—his hand on his lap, quietly discussing the fabulous restaurants in Paris, how dining there is "superior."

The rest of the dinner he talks about the days he spent in France, how he loves France, that the French are chic, know what they're doing. "In Europe, the clothes are beautiful, handmade. I buy most of my clothes now in Italy."

When dinner is over, we sip espressos, and I'm surprised how comfortable I feel with him. I ask him how he got started in diamonds.

He pauses, as if not sure he wants to reveal himself. Then he tells me that at fourteen, he worked in his uncle Ted's jewelry store in Toledo. "I was very poor, and I had to work to get things. One day a very beautiful young woman came to the store. She was wearing a large diamond ring, and she was so beautiful, so haughty, and at that moment I knew I wanted to buy and sell diamonds like that. Finding rare diamonds is a challenge, and even then I loved a challenge. It's all I've ever wanted to do. Except maybe sing."

"How interesting." I'm moved by his confession, his boylike wistfulness. "I always wanted to be a novelist, and performer. Anyway, I paint. I have a dealer and I hope to eventually have a show of my paintings. I'm working on paintings of women inside boxes."

A lady selling gardenias stops at our table. She carries a big basket of them. The combo has resumed playing Cole Porter tunes.

"I'll take all you have," Marv says to the lady, and drops a $50 bill in her basket. She puts the gardenias in a cellophane bag and gives it to me.

"Thank you, Marv." I inhale the sweet aroma of the flowers. "I love gardenias."

He looks at me as if he's making up his mind about something. Then he glances at his watch. "Let's go to my place. I'll show you my art."

I'm taken off guard. I feel flustered, clutching the bag of gardenias, thinking, *Okay, the big man bought me dinner and gardenias, but going to his apartment shows too much interest at this point. "Be unavailable,"* I remember Emily warning. "Well, I have an early deadline in the morning. Not tonight," I say.

"Sure, another time," he says, and I feel his warmth fade into a sudden formality.

I stand, wobbling slightly. My knee is stiff. Sometimes when I stand too fast, I lose my balance. But he takes my hand and we go outside, where the valet drives up with Marv's black Mercedes convertible.

In the car, he turns on his CD player and sings along with Frank Sinatra in a smoky voice, as if he's onstage. I lean back, watching the moon blow up into a baroque pearl, and the night is suddenly warm, as if maybe there's going to be an earthquake. At a stop sign he holds my hand, and I feel as if my skin is electrified.

"The stars are like diamonds."

"They'll be gone soon," he says, sounding morose.

"Stars last forever."

"Nothing lasts forever." He squeezes my hand.

He stops his car in front of my building and walks me to the door. I'm carrying the bag of gardenias and we walk slowly.

At the door, I fumble for my key and open the door. In the overhead lamplight, his eyes appear almost hazel, and up close, tiny silver hairs like threads are in his thick, dark eyebrows. He kisses me lightly on the mouth, and just the feel of his kiss, his taste, makes me breathless. Oh my God, I'm lavishing the kiss.

He grins, as if he knows that I'm dying for him. "I want to do that again soon, Anny."

"Me too," I say, my heart beating fast.

"I'll call you, Anny."

I rush into the apartment lobby and float upstairs.

I don't turn on the lights, wanting to keep the night as long as I can, feeling as if I've been struck by some voodoo, standing on the edge of a high mountain, trying not to fall off. I can't believe this is happening—this magic, this absolute stunning chemistry. I float the gardenias in a huge bowl of water, inhaling their sweet scent.

At the window, I sit on my favorite leather chair, watching the stars blinking silver in the vast dark sky, thinking about the night—wondering if he really thought I'd go to his apartment. Or if he thought I'd sleep with him. Or am I so out of the loop with dating that I acted like a silly schoolgirl? But no way am I ready for sex. Not to mention he has this ex-wife thing. Still, there's something underneath all that, something that makes me swoon, something about his quest for beauty that seems vulnerable, so like a young boy dreaming of a shiny new car. Yet, some wild chemistry that hasn't happened to me since I met Donald forty-five years ago at a party, and we danced all night, happened. "I'll love you forever," Donald had said. He meant it until he met Conchita.

The streets are suddenly devoid of traffic. But the stars are still blinking, and I feel exhilarated by the new day, and seeing Marv again.

After I take my baby aspirin, Citracal, and Lipitor, I get into bed, the scent of the gardenias on the nightstand tantalizing my senses.

I wrap myself in my old down comforter and turn off the light. I love this part of night—the quiet. And as I slowly slide into sleep, his kisses still on my mouth, butterflies in my stomach, my dreams take me to unresolved places, and I watch myself in lost events, feel feelings that I had buried, dreams full of butterflies and the scent of gardenias.

Chapter 6

God, please don't make me love Marv Rothstein. It's two weeks later and he hasn't called. No matter how many times I assure myself that he's a rat, and not for me, I can't stop thinking about him, obsessing, wondering, what did I do wrong? Every minute I check and recheck my messages, assuring myself that he's away, or some emergency happened. "He must have been called away on business," I explain to the girls and to Emily.

It's a sunny afternoon and I'm at the dog park in Berkeley with Emily, walking Fred. We walk briskly, trying to keep up with Fred, who's running along the edge of the park, chasing balls. In black leggings, a white tank top, and tennis shoes, Emily appears much younger than her forty-one years. Her jet-black hair is worn in a long ponytail and tied by a red ribbon. Emily recites her latest scone recipe, her voice rising

above the sound of the wind. Her baking business is successful, and she has two new partners.

"You're not listening," she says, looking at me with exas-
peration. Her eyes are black, and her tilted nose and full
mouth are so like her father's.

"Chocolate and raisins," I snap. "I heard you."

"Your mind is on that Marv louse. Men who come on
to you and then don't call are louses. For two weeks you've
been like a sick schoolgirl waiting for his stupid call. 'Nothing lasts,' he said. So listen to the louse. With him, nothing
more than a moment lasts. Answer the other JDates. Meet a
suitable husband."

"I don't want another husband. I have a career."

"A column that's about to go," she says, a sympathetic expression on her face, the way a parent looks at an unrealistic child.

She throws another ball to Fred, calling his name. She
holds his binky, which is a ratty cloth duck he's had since
they picked him up at the rescue farm, and a peanut-butter-
covered bone.

"Anyway, he could be away," I say, sitting down on the
bench, Emily next to me.

"He has a cell phone, Mom. Away with who? His ex-wife?"

"No. They're friends."

"Mom. You're smarter than that. You're doing the same
thing you did with Dad. It was obvious that he had someone.
He was never home and you were always making excuses.
Plus you had a sexless marriage. You told me that."

"Don't lecture me."

"You buried your head in the sand. Mom, don't let the divorce hurt your chances to meet someone wonderful. Go for someone great like Ryan. He's cool, and an artist. You have more in common."

"He's a friend."

"Stop with the friend crap. He's wonderful and he adores you. I can tell. Harry likes him too."

"Anyway, he's only fifty-four and I'm sixty-five."

"What's wrong with that? You always said age is only a number. You just like Marv because you know he's emotionally unavailable. You always want what you can't have, and don't want what you can have."

"So how are you and Harry?" I ask after long silence.

"You mean, why isn't Harry marrying me?"

"I didn't—say that."

"You don't have to."

"You've lived together six years. You're over forty and he's fifty. What's the problem? Why doesn't Harry marry you? He's one of those commitment phobics. If he hasn't married you now, he won't—"

"Chill out!" Emily shouts, her face all red. "You're always pushing. Harry doesn't want marriage! Anyway, what's so great about marriage? Do you think I want to go through what you've gone through?"

"I'm sorry, Emily. I want you to be happy. I feel guilty that I caused you so much pain."

She bites her bottom lip, looking at me with pleading, emotional eyes. "Mom, I don't want you to be old and alone. Wait till you're sick and pee in your bed and have no one by your side."

As I watch her brush Fred with her special dog brush, talking to him in their own special language, I feel sad, remembering Emily as a child, lovingly brushing her father's Arabian horses. And how I wish I could go back in time and parent her over again, be more loving, more attentive. Since I started therapy, I see so clearly how distant I was, how I was only into my painting and writing and dreams, ignoring Emily as my mother had ignored me. And I wonder if adult mothers and daughters can retrieve that childhood together. If they can rise above the past.

Emily pours bottled water into the little plastic bowl she carries in her bag, places an ice cube in the bowl of water. Fred laps it up, then she gives him a cookie with peanut butter on it. We walk in silence toward the car, her chin pointed up, mine down.

In the car, we don't talk. Fred lies along my lap. At the BART station, the daylight gone now, Emily gives me a bag of scones. "Call me when you get home," she says.

I get out of the car, and then she drives away.

By the time I get home it's almost evening. I turn on the track lights, and they make a popping sound as they flicker on. Emily upset me, but I can't stop remembering the feel of

Marv's kiss. He's probably away, I assure myself. And besides, we only had one date.

I turn on the boom box to the classical station, listening to Bach and trying to relax. I make a salad, then watch the news. After dinner, I try to work on my boxes, but I can't. I'm feeling confused, remembering his last words to me, "I'll call you," and wondering, why hasn't he?

At my computer I write notes about my date with Marv, trying to see what went wrong, recording every detail I can remember, his every silence, gesture. Usually, the only way I can get my feelings out is to write about them.

He sits low in his Mercedes convertible and remarks three times that his seats are heated and isn't it great to have such a car?

His ego is full of money. He loves money, and what it can buy. He loves perfection. He lives on the outside of things, like a strange bug that crawls along the surface of the ground, never going below it. "The stars will be gone soon," he said. Does he only exist in the moment, and then retreat into his castles of diamonds and high places? Does sex mean love to him? Love mean sex? Does it ever come together?

Trying to break into some answers, I continue writing about him, how he looked, what he ate. I call him Mr. X.

Mr. X walks like he owns the ground, and immediately I feel breathless, like my bones are on fire, as if my heart opened. He searches for the next perfect diamond.

Under the stars he kissed me, and it felt like he was swallowing me. I felt his heart beating against mine, and I knew that with one more kiss I'd go back with him to his apartment and never want to leave.

I stop writing. Then it dawns on me. Mr. X is my column. He's perfect. He's smart, successful, and clinging to his youth. Mr. X is like so many boomer-plus guys and he will be the poster boy for the mishaps of the Viagra generation—men who use Viagra like candy, who think it will bring them youth, who prevent intimacy. Yes, everything is for a reason. For sure the date was worth it. Meant to be. And this moment, with this decision I feel alive, redeemed, and inspired.

For the next two hours I write my first Mr. X column, concealing Marv's distinct physical appearance by making Mr. X shorter with darker hair and a receding hairline. I expand on our date, describing the details, our dialogue, exactly what he was wearing, that he walks fast but not lifting his feet, and that between exuberant phrases about his travels, with detailed descriptions, he'd pause, as if reflecting, or deciding if he wanted to continue. Every move calculated. I describe his elegant manners, his slick perfection, and his moments of charm. I write about this wonderful evening, ending it after the kiss. "I'll call you," he says.

I print the column out, and after I edit the hard copy, then type in the corrections, it's ready to go to Monica. I like its energy. It's real. I feel electrified.

I write Monica a pitch, proposing a series of columns about a sixty-plus woman looking for a Mr. X: *I propose The Viagra Diaries, a series about love after sixty.*

I e-mail the column and the pitch to Monica. It's done. By now it's late and the room is cold.

Slowly, I stretch my arms, feeling as if my career just took a turn. I get ready for bed and fall right into sleep, dreaming that I'm dancing the tango with Marv. I wear a black, short dress, a high slit on the side, a pink rose in the side of my hair twisted into a long chignon. He dances perfectly, but I'm stepping on his feet, and leaning too forward, but he holds me tight and guides me into the steps.

The next morning, first thing, Monica calls.

"I like your proposal for The Viagra Diaries," she says. "The Mr. X column is fun, and I think a series about boomer dating will be great."

"I'm delighted," I say, relieved and thrilled that she likes it. I feel as though everything has changed again, and to the better.

"I'll run it next week. Forget the Seniors on the Run. It's a bore."

"I agree."

"Bring our paper a Pulitzer."

"Sure, no problem," I say with a laugh.

"Get to work. Find the next Mr. X."

"Will do."

"You can't disappoint your readers."

After I hang up, I log on to JDate and retrieve the e-mails

that other men had sent me. I read several, deciding to reply to a therapist and author of a book called *Happy Women*, and a man who professes to be a billionaire who wants a simple life.

I reply, then wait.

Chapter 7

I t's a week later and Ryan is home from his shoot in Holland. I'm meeting him at a gallery opening for his friend Manny Futz, a classmate from the Chicago Art Institute. It is evening and I arrive by taxi at the Solar Gallery on Mission Street. Decked out tonight, I'm wearing high, black, shiny leather boots that I found at a thrift shop, a black leather jacket with silver zippers, and jeans I painted flowers on.

Ryan greets me at the entrance with a big hug. "Anny, it's so great to see you." He kisses me on each cheek.

"You too," I say, glad to see him. He's a little taller than I am, about five feet nine. His gold hair hangs long in the back, and he has the bluest eyes I've ever seen. He wears a black jacket, T-shirt, snug jeans, and his usual hiking boots.

I adjust my fedora over my hair, following Ryan up the crooked stairs, into the gallery. Once an old tamale warehouse, the gallery sits above a well-known Mexican restaurant, and the delicious smell of Mexican food sifts up the stairs. It's a sensational space, almost three thousand square feet with bumpy, gray concrete floors. High industrial windows overlook the Bay and the San Francisco ballpark. Track lights dangle strategically over the massive paintings. Hot Latino music bursts loudly from the speakers, and the gallery is crowded with art groupies wearing fake fur, with green hair and clutching iPhones. Gorgeous young waiters serve champagne and red wine in plastic cups. Pretty young girls wearing black, with red lips, clay necklaces, and high boots, stand in groups, texting and talking on their phones.

After we greet and congratulate Manny, Ryan and I move from drawings to paintings, each with variations of dots. The paintings are massive with grids of juicy-fruit-colored dots. He moves closer to a painting. His firm body is graceful. His hands are slouched into his pockets, his shoulders back. In a streetwise kind of way, he's handsome. There's something cool about him, mixed with something dark, deeply private.

We stand by a hexagon construction titled *Nocturnal City*. Next to us a couple discusses the painting.

"Dots," says the man, standing close to the painting. His comb-over is dyed red and he wears a too tight leather jacket and baggy jeans.

"So many dots. They say twenty-five thousand," says the woman next to him. She stands close to the painting, her long, red fingernail counting the dots. She wears black leggings and a black Harvard T-shirt. Her tiny face is very white and her lips are very red. "So lyrical."

"Dots are dots," he says with a shrug.

"So postmodern, so—"

"Postshit."

"Well, Seurat used dots," the woman persists.

"Pointillism," snaps the man.

"Anny, what do you think?" Ryan asks in his lilting Irish accent. His eyes are questioning. He has grown a narrow mustache above his full, sensual mouth. The back of his hair hangs over the collar of his black turtleneck sweater.

"I think the work is self-conscious. It doesn't move me like van Gogh moves me. Or the way your photographs of children in Ethiopia move me. These paintings are—pretentious," I say. "Art documents life. It asks questions, expresses the human condition, and shouldn't be made for rich patrons. I find the dots derivative of so many artists—Robert Ryan-Martin, Roy Lichtenstein—"

"Exactly," Ryan says, smiling, his eyes sparkling. "Futz uses dots to tell the story of our culture. He plays with cynicism, makes fun of the art world. Art is a lot of things, Anny—it's not one thing. It's everything."

"Well, I hate the dots. It's prissy snobbery catering to the phonies who need dots on their walls to feel cultured."

He laughs. "C'mon. Let's go to dinner. After I'll come up and see your boxes."

Arm in arm we venture into the rain.

After a fun, wonderful dinner of pasta, we're at my apartment. I make coffee and ask him to critique my boxes and paintings.

"I like the woman with the high-heel shoes and silver hair, standing in the box." He points to a medium-size canvas propped against the wall. "She's got attitude. It's great."

"Really? It's new. You like it?"

He looks directly at me. "She's not fragile," he continues, a thoughtful expression on his intelligent, Irish face. He stands so close to me I see the black, thin rims around his corneas, and the blue is the color of cornflowers.

"I see her in control. She's beautiful and interesting and sexy."

"Good, I hope so."

"Like you, Anny. Nothing about you is fragile."

His stare makes me uncomfortable.

"Who's the shadowy man in the painting?" he asks, pointing to the man in the corner of the canvas.

I flush. "My fantasy love. He's a recurrent obsession."

"It's your obsessions that make your paintings interesting. Keep working on these."

"Obsessions are good, I guess."

"I have plenty myself," he says.

"I'd love to hear about them sometime."

As he tells me about the new Nikon camera he just bought, about the different lenses he uses to explore light, my mind wanders to the night last winter when I had chest pains and thought I was having a heart attack. I woke him up at 2:00 a.m., and he drove me to the emergency room. He stayed with me until the doctors assured me it was only something I ate, and then he took the long way home, calming my nerves with stories about his youth in Ireland.

"I can show you how to use the new lens, Anny. You could take better photographs—maybe integrate them into your paintings." He removes a drop cloth from a painting of boxes, leaning along the wall. "They're wonderfully odd," he says, "especially the paper butterflies—trying to fly," he muses. "I like the thin needles hanging from gold threads, the tiny, dangling boxes from tiny dolls inside."

"I believe that our truths exist in our unconscious. So the images I use are from there. I steal myself."

"As long as you don't steal your soul," he says, intently looking at me.

"How can one do that?"

"By watching and not living."

"Let's drink our coffee," I say, uncomfortable that he sees into me.

On the sofa, we sit next to each other, drinking coffee, eating scones, and quietly talking. He is concerned about his new photographs of stray dogs that he's doing for the magazine. He wants to capture their loneliness.

I tell him about my Mr. X column, which will be published next Thursday. "My editor is excited, and I have huge hopes that it will turn my career around."

"Who is Mr. X?"

I hesitate. "He's based on a man I met." I blurt out the story of my date with Marv, how taken I was with him. "He wanted me to go to his apartment afterward, but I—well, I'm scared. You know my story. Anyway, I was very attracted to him, and I thought he was to me, and he hasn't called—maybe I should have slept with him—"

"You don't want an asshole who doesn't call," Ryan says, looking annoyed.

"He's very busy. He deals in million-dollar diamonds. Anyway, it's been three weeks now. He travels a lot—"

"He's a fool. Meet someone who knows how wonderful you are."

"Well, I just thought I'd tell you. I just wonder if I did something wrong? If I acted silly when he wanted me to go to his apartment? He just wanted to show me his art." I pause. "He says I remind him of valentines—"

"Anny, you did what was right for you. Don't ever do less." Ryan pauses. "You know I'd call you back right away."

"Ryan. I'm flattered—"

"What do you think about me?"

"I like you a lot. But I can never think of us that way—"

"Never say never."

"My God. We sound like a movie." I laugh and try to drown out the sudden silence between us. But Ryan seems lost in thought.

He stands. "It's late. I have to go."

At the door we hug lightly. "I bought you a van Gogh catalog in Amsterdam. I'll drop it off tomorrow."

"Thank you. I can't wait to read it," I say, moved by his thoughtful gift. I watch him hurry downstairs, surprised by his confession.

Chapter 8

Marv doesn't call. But it doesn't matter, I assure myself; my first Mr. X column is a hit. I start receiving fan mail almost immediately: women over sixty e-mail their personal stories about meeting emotionally unavailable men like Mr. X. Some write that they hope they'll be the one to change him. I'm thrilled. Anyway, Monica loves the Mr. X columns and tells me that The Viagra Diaries *is* gaining a larger audience. She offers me more space. I have hopes that the column is taking off. But without Marv, I can't write about Mr. X. I need new material, new hot boomer guys, so I start scouring JDate for boomers. *Plenty of sexy, charismatic diamond-dealing fish in the sea,* I tell myself, hoping to forget Marv Rothstein.

I line up more sixty-plus men I meet at bereavement groups, funerals, fund-raisers, all wanting to be interviewed—

a seventy-five-year-old screenwriter who schleps an Emmy that he won thirty years ago, in his car, a sixty-one-year-old German paratrooper with blond, curly hair and a huge, square jaw who doesn't believe in bathing. I meet them at Starbucks or for drinks. Most of the sixty-plus men, even the sharp ones, are looking for that young dream, something they missed in their life. They go to Brazil for face-lifts, buy new cars, and want to date twenty-five-year-old Swedish maids. Viagra has spoiled these men. Many of the men had for various reasons given up on sex, until Viagra swooped in, and suddenly all they want to do is go to "Viagra Falls" and "sow their oats." What seventy-year-old still has oats left to sow? Many people wonder, but I believe everything is possible at every age, and that Viagra is one of the greatest things since the cure of polio. It's possible that a committed relationship is simply different after sixty. Or, more likely, that a committed relationship is different after Viagra. Maybe it becomes about the sex and not the intimacy? Or, maybe both.

My second column is titled "Men-Oh-Pause," about a sixty-nine-year-old hypochrondriac with sleep apnea. It hits a nerve and I get tons of e-mails from boomer men complaining that I'm an angry bitch. "Now we've got controversy," Monica says. She gives me a raise and I pay off some bills. God, I love writing this column, and love the recognition— neighbors stopping me in the street, or strangers recognizing me from my photo, and then raving about the column. I feel alive. I'm writing about ageism, and what I believe in.

I write snippets about my meetings, give them titles, and develop them later for future columns: "Is He Still with the Ex?" "Herpes or Hermès?" "Boomer Bad Boy," and many others. Most of the men I interview want to talk about Viagra and their sex lives and are shockingly candid.

Meet Max, Boomer Clean Freak: He's a seventy-four-year-old successful lawyer. God forbid you get a spot on his new, black, shiny Smart car. He raves about the sound system he had "specially installed" for his car. He collects cars and women and is pretty slick looking. Only he's afraid of bugs. He won't touch the menu or share your guacamole dip. It might have germs. He emphasizes that before he makes love with a woman he checks out her body "to make sure she's not infested."

Boomer Cheapskate: Mel is a sixty-year-old journalist. He's slight, with a face that was probably once handsome but is now rubbery, froglike. He wears a Sam Spade–type hat and thrift clothes that smell like dusty boxes. He doesn't have a car but takes the bus to meet you for the early-bird special at the Indian restaurant. With his mouth full of rice he grumbles that his career is a "fucking mess." He moans, "The only way to make money at my age is to win the lottery or break a hip at Safeway."

Boomer Jerk: Walter Blumberg is a sixty-two-year-old surgeon who specializes in penile implants. He wears a mullet, which looks like a rat attacked to his small head, and such thick glasses that his eyes appear as dots. He's been divorced three times and can't find the "right woman." He spent a year in prison for tax evasion. He wears surgical clothes and repeats that he was Mr. Orange County in college, and that the women are still after him for his looks. "I'm a good-looking doctor who makes money, so every yenta is after me. They're oldies. I want my woman to be no older than thirty-two, smart, with a pair of real knockers," he rants. "At my age, I'm not going to marry some gray-haired woman who spends my money on breast implants when she'll be in diapers in ten years anyway. What I want to know is, who's changing my diaper? All the woman want is our money."

"Not all women," I interject. "And that's because most women are discriminated against." Walter looks at me as if I were from another planet.

Jim Wilson is good-looking, seventy-five, and fit. He drives a ten-year-old Ford, owns a lot of property, and is a widower. He wears schlumpy, baggy khaki pants and a wrinkled shirt. He has the first nickel he ever earned, he brags, and his suspicious, tiny eyes check you out as if he's deciding to purchase you or not. "Do you live in a condo, or house?" he asks.

"I rent," I say.

"I have a time-share in Mexico and a thousand acres in Montana. I need a woman who owns property. I'm tired of being Santa Claus."

I stop writing. It's almost noon and I have a two o'clock meeting at Starbucks with the sixty-six-year-old sailboat designer and widower who had contacted me earlier. I call him to confirm our date. He answers right away.

"How will I know you?" I ask. "You don't have a photo posted."

"They say I look like Clint."

"Klimt? The painter?"

"Eastwood," he impatiently replies. "This is why I can't put my photo up. I don't want the older women stalking me."

"Sure," I say. "Well, I'll be wearing black. I'm tall, with long brown and gray-streaked hair."

I arrive at Starbucks an hour early, planning on doing some work. I stand in line. Men and women, some wearing gym clothes and baseball hats, order drinks. This Starbucks is near my apartment and I come here every day, after writing and my two-mile walk along Fisherman's Wharf, where I watch the sailboats and fishermen catching crabs in big nets. I love the kids here. Angela, a pretty blond girl who laughs all the time, waves.

"Hello, Anny," Justin says. "Same?"

"Cappuccino, tall, dry inside, nonfat foam on top."

"You got it," Justin says, writing my name on a cup. He's a handsome African-American man about twenty-five. So sweet. He calls out, "Anny's drink," to Jessica, who waves. She's tiny with black, shiny hair cut blunt to her chin. Often in the past she's given me free drinks. She's an art student at the Academy of Art. On the wall they've framed my column "Seniors at Starbucks."

I find a table in the back, next to the window. Today lots of people are on bicycles, or sitting outside, talking and drinking coffee. Polk Street is narrow with bumpy sidewalks and surrounded by health-food stores, expensive markets, cafés, but mixed in are funky, old bookstores and old flats above more coffeehouses. Tour buses, almost too wide for the street, slowly go by.

I sip the foam from the top of my coffee, enjoying it. I work on notes for my next column, "Even Ugly Men Are Jerks," then take notes in my notebook. The sounds of coffee beans grinding, and of the kids behind the counter calling out names of drinks, mingle with the ringing of cell phones and the clicking of keyboards.

I look up from my writing and I see a man at the counter who is tall and slender like Marv. My heart leaps. But then he turns, and I realize it isn't him. I resume writing. Until a little past two, a tan, tall man, with a body like Gumby's and a head of high, pale tan hair, walks in. I watch him get a coffee, then he walks right to me and sits down.

"Anny?"

I nod.

"Dick Knight," he says, his tan eyes openly looking me up and down. He smiles, revealing even, too perfect, veneered teeth. Close up his tan looks sprayed on. He has a long, narrow face and a sharp widows peak.

"I Googled you," he says, slurping his drink. "I read your columns online. You seem angry with men."

"Only with the jerks."

He laughs, as if he's not one of them.

We shoot the breeze about what we like to do, eat, places to go, films. I find out he's a Republican for the religious right. Warming up now, he tells me how "rotten" his marriage was and it's time for "numero uno," he repeats, his fists pounding his thin chest. "My wife was frigid, and for forty-two years I put in my dues," he says. He pauses. "I'm a deep person—highly sensitive. I want a woman who looks like Pamela Anderson with brains."

"Gotcha," I say, thinking I'll call the column "Widow's Prick."

"I've never been with a woman your age."

"Whoopee," I say. "We have vaginas and everything."

He frowns and looks around the room.

"So how did your wife die?"

He affects a sympathetic expression. "She was at the beauty parlor, having extensions sewn into her hair. When she got up, she tripped on a cord, broke her hip. She was a klutz. Died from complications."

"When did your wife die?"

"Three days ago," he replies.

I glance at my watch. "Whoops. I have a deadline. I have to go."

"I can tell you're neurotic," he says, looking nasty. "That crazy hat. Painted jeans."

"I also wear Spanx," I say, getting up.

• • •

Later, at home, I write "Widow's Prick," and e-mail it to Monica. I have more e-mails and fan mail. I write lists of new ideas and themes about aging and ageism. *Sixty is the new forty, but is it?* I write. *What's wrong with sixty being sixty? What's wrong with celebrating our age, and who we really are?*

My cell phone rings, interrupting my train of thought. I don't answer it, but it keeps ringing. I don't recognize the number on the screen, but the caller won't let up so I answer.

"Hello, Anny. This is Marv Rothstein."

I hold the phone tight, my heart beating hard, and I can't breathe.

"Anny, did I get you at a bad time?"

"I'm . . . writing," I say, trying to sound casual.

"I've wanted to call you, but the day after I saw you, I had an emergency business deal in Zimbabwe to find a very perfect canary diamond. Then I've been in Belgium, London, and Paris." He pauses. "Anny, I've thought about you."

Silence. I'm trembling.

"I thought of sending flowers, but I wasn't sure you wanted to hear from me as you ran off so fast. Anyway, I want to see you." He pauses again. "Can you go out tomorrow night?"

"Well . . . yes, I can."

"I thought we'd go to dinner. I'll pick you up at eight." He pauses. "I can't wait to see you, Valentine."

After I hang up, I'm dying. Here I have been using him as a model for Mr. X, trashing him to Janet, and Lisa, and I'm feeling embarrassed; at the same time, I'm ten feet off the ground. My heart is beating so hard it feels as if it were going to go through my chest, and—*oh my God, my hair*, I think, deciding to go to Rose and have my hair blown and shaped, and definitely a manicure . . . oh my God. What to wear? Yes, the new black pants—black turtleneck. Simple.

I call Janet. She answers on the first ring.

"So I'm going out with him again."

"Him who?"

"Marv Rothstein."

"Hey, honey! Great!"

"I feel kind of embarrassed. I had sworn him off, but as soon as I hear his voice, bam, I'm off and running. Plus, I'm writing about him."

"Honey, go for it. He's hot, rich, and probably gets it up! Stop obsessing."

"I already can tell he's bad news. He has other women. I'm sure of it, and I don't really know him."

"You know enough to write about him. Honey, go for the diamond ring. Ignore the rest. Call me after the date."

Chapter 9

Wouldn't you know it? It's an hour before Marv is picking me up and I'm having a bad-hair day. I'm blowing my hair, trying to smooth it out, telling myself that this is only a date. In fact, it's business. After all, isn't he the man who acted as if I were the only woman on earth, then didn't call? Still, look what happened. I have a column that's taking off, and my career is changing. All because of him.

I turn off the hair dryer, shake my hair so it falls loose. Then I clip a tiny black feather on the side.

The phone rings. It's Janet.

"So did you put the gray shadow on?"

"Shadow, moisturizer, perfume—you name it. I'm done."

"Good, honey. Show him you like him. This guy's got the bucks. Don't listen to cranky Lisa. Honey, enjoy." Janet sighs.

"Last night I went out with the sixty-year-old Persian count I told you about. Gorgeous. Suave. Smells like Neiman Marcus. He wined and dined me at Scala's. After dinner he took me to his suite at the Ritz-Carlton. *Oy vay.* We're going great guns, and, bam, poor man has a teeny weenie. Plus, he has allergies. Every second with the nasal spray and the snorts. So be glad you're going out with a fox."

"I'll call you tomorrow," I say, laughing.

One more time I spin in the mist of Chanel perfume, smoothing my hair. Exactly at eight, Marv calls on my cell phone. He's downstairs. Just the sound of his velvet voice makes me crazy—and I suddenly wish I weren't wearing my Walgreens cotton underwear with the butterflies on it. After my divorce I didn't exactly feel sexy. I wore underwear like the Amish.

"Be right down," I say, monitoring my voice.

I hurry down the stairs, all my reserve gone, holding tightly to the rail so I don't fall, and my heart is beating fast. God, there he is, my Mr. X, standing by his black Mercedes convertible, watching as I walk toward him. He looks real swank wearing all black—a black turtleneck sweater, and a long black overcoat, black jeans, his silver hair slicked. I'm breathless. He looks better than I had remembered.

"Hello, Anny," he softly says, his appraising eyes on me, in one blink taking all of me in. He hugs me, says how glad he is to see me, and politely helps me into the car.

He drives into the traffic. The music is on, and Tony Bennett sings "I Left My Heart in San Francisco." It's a cold night, and his fur seats are heated.

Just sitting next to him arouses me, and I'm feeling breathless.

"They say it's going to rain—"

"You smell good," he says.

"Green tea. You smell good too."

"So we both smell good," he says, laughing. "I thought we'd dine at Pasha's. They serve the best Middle Eastern food in town."

"Sounds good." Spicy food does me in, but no way do I want to tell him that.

"Tonight, we'll take up where we left off."

"Well, we'll see," I say, thinking, *What nerve.*

Then he sings to the song, his low, smooth voice enunciating each word. At stop signs, he holds my hand. God, this man has me going, and I'm feeling this glow I haven't felt in years, the kind you feel when desire overwhelms you and you're on the brink of sex. Something has happened between us. I can feel it.

The headwaiter, Raja, makes a big fuss over Marv and leads us to the corner table in the back. This Persian music is going wild, real sexy, and candles are lit everywhere. This man is something. As if we were just together, he orders my Stoli over with three green olives, and the same for him. Then he orders all these spicy kebab things on sticks, and we drink up a storm.

"I thought you drank Cutty Sark," I say.

"I want to drink what you drink. I really like you, Anny."

"How do you know after one time?"

"I know. I wish we had met years ago."

"How would that be different?" I ask.

"Youth. We'd be younger." He looks gloomy.

"Age has nothing to do with youth," I say, disappointed with his answer and feeling a growing pit in my stomach.

He smiles. "Anny, you're sweet. You're like a rose in bloom." He blinks. "Did you think about me?"

"I want to be mysterious, so I'm not going to tell you."

He grins. "You *are* mysterious."

"So you've been divorced for seven years," I say, eating spicy eggplant. "And in all this time, didn't you meet someone you liked?"

He shrugs. "I dated one woman in Grass Valley. She had a house with a pool. A nice figure. I spent weekends with her. The sex was better than what I'd had. But she didn't do anything but wait for me to see her on weekends. It didn't work out."

The rest of the dinner is a blur, and I'm barely eating. All my reservations slowly recede. The sensuous music is rising and we're feeling no pain. We're laughing at nothing, flirting like teenagers in heat, saying nothing important or profound.

I never thought at my stage of life I'd act so drippy, doing this Bette Davis thing—shaking my hair, dropping my wrist, laughing at his silly story about something his granddaughter said to him, and pretending that he hadn't just told the same story ten minutes ago. I feel sexual arousal like I've never felt before, as if all my nerves are open and no one else is in the room and there's only us. And as he tells me about the perfect diamonds he's bought and sold, everything about him turns me on: his manicured nails, the texture of his olive, smooth skin, the yellow flecks floating around the rims of his dark eyes, his sultry mouth that goes in an upward line, and his slicked, silky hair. I'm hooked.

When the dinner is over, he invites me to see his place. "I want to show you my art. I think you'll like it."

"Well, it's kind of late."

"Oh, come on. A cognac, a drink, and a few kisses."

"Don't scare me," I say, trying to sound oh so cool. Anyway, this might be a column, I remind myself.

In the car, he's got the Tony Bennett tapes on again, and he's singing along in this raspy voice, as if he were in a nightclub. I'm telling myself a few kisses won't hurt, and so what's wrong with going to his place?

He stops the car on Nob Hill. He lives in this gorgeous high-rise, the kind you see in those magazines with wealthy men lounging on a Corbusier chair. Nob Hill features the

Fairmont and Mark Hopkins Hotels, opulent high-rises, town houses, elegant restaurants. Rows of trees line the narrow streets, and doormen stand guard at every façade, wearing red jackets and gold whistles around their necks. Cable-car tracks make a steady buzzing sound.

Hand in hand, we take the elevator to the twenty-eighth floor. The elevator stops at the penthouse and Marv opens the door. Immediately this small, white dog, as tiny as a sock, encircles his feet.

"This is Honey," he says. "Isn't she adorable?" Honey weighs about four pounds—a cotton ball with two black eyes.

"She's adorable," I say, petting her. Honey snaps at me. I pull back.

"She just has to get to know you," he explains. "She's a show dog. Highly sensitive."

"Your view is spectacular." I admire the panoramic view of the city and the Golden Gate Bridge. Floor-to-ceiling windows surround the living and dining area, elegantly decorated with ultramodern furniture and antiques. "Wow."

"Pretty good for a boy from Toledo." He looks pleased with himself. He turns on a switch, and recessed lights shaped like stars drop a low, pink glow, and Frank Sinatra softly plays.

Like a starstruck kid, he animatedly tells me about the celebrities who live in his building. "I'm supposed to meet Christie Hefner." He pauses. "Cognac?"

"Lovely," I say, admiring the framed photographs of Marv with Madonna, Bono, Sting and his wife. The women are haughty looking, and beautiful. "These photographs are amazing. Are they clients?"

He nods, pouring the cognac into two large, bowl-shaped glasses. "Those are only a few. I've sold diamonds to the most beautiful women in the world. They're all magnificent. They're as perfect as the diamonds I sold them."

"What is this award for?" A huge gold plaque has Marv's name on it, for his "goodwill."

"I invested money in a diamond mine in Nigeria."

"Wow." I sit on the beige suede sectional, facing the view, glancing about the room. Though beautiful and obviously reflecting wealth and success, the decor has the too studied look of a slick interior designer: wide, beige suede chairs and no bookcases filled with books. But there are marble sculptures of lovers, and colorful abstract paintings, and everywhere orchids are in bloom. Everything is neat, beautiful, as if anything short of beauty is not tolerated. So different from my studio apartment cluttered with books and papers and paintings. Everything is polished and arranged, as if his real essence is hidden.

"I love good cognac," he says, sitting next to me. He places two coasters shaped like shells on the white marble coffee table, then gives me my glass. He inhales the cognac, sighing and closing his eyes. For a second, he's quiet, as if the cognac deserves a moment of reverence. While the strong aroma makes my eyes water, and I'm still dizzy from the night, I attempt a few sips.

"My first wife and I used to go on wine-tasting trips," he says, then sips the cognac. "In Paris we'd buy cognac and wine. Our son, Maurice, was born there."

"Sounds romantic."

"It was," he says, a wistful expression on his face. "Paris is for lovers, for passion." He twirls the cognac in his glass, looking faraway, then drinks it.

"I've always wanted to go to Paris," I say, then sip my drink. "When I was young, I dreamed of living in Paris, painting, writing."

"Didn't you go with your husband?" He looks at me intently. Underneath his steady gaze, I feel him thinking, figuring out.

"No," I say with a sigh. "He was busy making money, and I was going to—art school. Anyway, it doesn't matter," I quickly say, feeling uncomfortable.

He suddenly looks tense. "My second ex-wife, Debra, would only let me have sex with her on Monday nights. She didn't like sex. I wanted it all the time. So she divorced me."

"How long were you married?" I ask, aware that his flirtatious mood has changed to gloom.

"Twelve years to Debra," he quickly answers. "Fifteen years to Giselle." He sighs and looks morose. "Both gorgeous wives were frigid."

"But you're still friends with Debra you said? Or are you and she still—involved?"

He shrugs. "No. We don't sleep together. She helps me sometimes with business, with diamond sales."

Sighing heavily, as if the world were on his shoulders, he takes off his Gucci loafers and stretches out on the couch, his arm around my waist. I hold my breath so he won't feel the roll around my middle.

"Altoid?" he asks, slipping one into his mouth.

"No, thanks," I say. "The moon is so bright. Like a pearl, isn't it?"

Gently he pushes aside the wave falling into my eye. "You're lovely," he says softly. "Underneath your quirky cavalier is a sensitive woman."

"Marv, it's been so long since I—"

He gently takes me in his arms and kisses me. At first I'm resistant, but then I'm on fire, kissing him back, kissing passionately, our tongues exploring, hoping he doesn't feel the spot on the upper-right side of my mouth where a bad fall knocked out two back teeth. But I can't stop kissing him.

"You're sexy," he whispers, his fingers stroking my face.

"You think so?" I whisper into his mouth, my body pressing closer to his.

"I know so. You're different. A beautiful woman. You're the most interesting woman I've ever met. I want to make love to you."

"You do? How do you know?"

"I know. From the first time we met, I wanted to make love to you. You just know those things."

"You want to make love, or have sex?"

"Anny, you're the only woman I want to have sex with."

Suddenly, I felt confused, scared, and not sure. So I excuse myself to use the powder room.

"Use my bathroom," he says, leading me to a hallway. "Straight down the hall, through the bedroom."

The hallway is lit with a low light. Trembling from the kiss, I cross his massive master bedroom. The carpets are so thick I sink, and the walls are apricot silk. The huge king-size bed has a heavy coverlet. Above the bed is a large tapestry of India. His bathroom is like a Calvin Klein perfume ad—all white marble, really beautiful, a Jacuzzi tub, and a glass shower with white marble seats. The air is scented like pale mint. White orchids dangle from turquoise, handblown glass vases.

At the double sink, I turn on the water so he doesn't hear me, and I pick up the large glass bottle of men's cologne from Paris. I open the top, inhaling the subtle, elegant scent that he uses. Next, I open the medicine cabinet, looking at the vials of sleeping pills, diuretics, high-blood-pressure pills . . . and then I see a bottle of Viagra. I read the outside of the bottle. Dr. Morton Cohn prescribed 25 mg of thirty-two Viagra pills, dated three weeks ago. I count the pills. Only eleven are left. Which means that since we met, he's been seeing someone.

Stunned, and feeling deflated, the water still running, I put the bottle back, remembering when I found the bottle of Viagra in Donald's pocket. This is a bad sign. All the weeks

Marv didn't call, he'd been taking Viagra. "I've thought about you, only you," he said. No way do I want to be one of his women, part of his harem. I've had enough of that. As a pretty bubble dissolves in the wind, my fantasies suddenly dissolve.

I wash my hands with the scented soap and turn off the water. I smooth my hair and go back into the living room.

Marv is lying on the couch. "Come lie with me," he says, patting the cushion next to him.

I glance at my watch. "I'm sorry, Marv. I didn't realize it was late. So late. I have a deadline tomorrow—"

"Oh, Anny. Stay. I'll bring you home in the morning. Stay."

"No, sorry. I have to go home."

Slowly, his lips pressed tight, he puts on his shoes, then says that he has to bring Honey, as she needs her walk.

"Sure," I say, buttoning my jacket.

In the car, Honey in his lap, her small body pressed to his, there's this smoldering quiet—really tense. I want to tell him not to be hurt, that I'm not some young thing ready to pounce into his bed, and that I haven't had sex for a long time, and I want it to mean something, assuring myself that I'm doing the right thing. Why am I so upset then?

He stops his car in front of my building, gets out, and with an uptight expression on his face, he walks with me to my front door.

I fumble with my key, finally opening the door.

"Well, thank you, Marv," I say, kissing him on the cheek. "Another great time." He turns, and hurries to his car. He drives away.

Upstairs in my apartment, I turn on the switch, the track lights making a popping sound. I'm upset. I feel rejected, but then I'm remembering the Viagra pills, assuring myself that I did the right thing, and did he think that he'd squeeze me into some other woman's Monday-night slot? Certainly, he's a jerk, I assure myself. Yet there's still that something underneath his jerkiness that interests me.

Quickly, I undress, not even turning on the lights, wondering if maybe I missed something about him, something I didn't know. I decide to go on JDate, hoping his profile will give me some insight. I realize as my computer boots up that JDate records how often their clients are on the site.

I log on to the site, then as I scroll down to Marv's profile, I'm stunned. The site says Marv was on *twenty-two minutes after midnight.* Oh my God, he logged in fifteen minutes after he brought me home. Does this mean he was looking for a new date? Or is he responding to someone who had contacted him? Either way, I'm disappointed. Hurt. Rejected.

Wow. A rat. Emily is right. Now I'm furious. Quickly I write about the evening, writing every detail, what we ate, how he sounded, smelled, looked, down to his every word.

He's a fading diamond dealer who can't face old age. Mr. X carries his sex appeal like armor. While seeing one woman, he's on the prowl for another. And another. A sexually hungry, grabby boy, sexually rejected by two wives, wanting all the sex he can get.

I see the bottle of Viagra. Three weeks ago the prescription was filled. And why are there only eleven pills left?

I describe the tense quiet on the way home, his sulking because I didn't stay. I describe the hurt sound of his voice when he confided that his ex-wife would only let him have sex with her on Monday nights. I describe every detail of the date.

I title the column "He Called. Mr. X Is Back. Is He a Bad-Boy Boomer?"

When I finish writing, I e-mail the pages to Monica, and then I get ready for bed. I feel exhilarated by the column, and duped by him.

Now I'm really excited. I'm always excited when I get a story idea. I know that I'm onto something; I feel the energy.

Exhausted but excited, I'm in bed. I watch the dawn light float along the ceiling, listening to the traffic. I love the sounds of cars and motorcycles, of people going to destinations. As I watch the lights shape patterns along the walls, my thoughts turn to Marv again, recalling his deadpan expression, his busy silence. Something about him is unplugged, covered up—the too manicured nails, the too perfect decor, the lonely shine in the kitchen, the soft, modulated voice. Something hidden. Defensive.

As I slip into sleep, I hear the tango. I love the tango. It's about love.

Chapter 10

"Men are trolls with penises!" I say. "Fifteen minutes after he brought me home, he was on JDate trolling for new women."

Dr. Indira remains quiet. It's the next afternoon and I'm at therapy, lying on the couch, my feet hanging over the edge. Why can't she buy a longer couch? Dr. Indira sits behind me. I never see her during our sessions, but I know her every silence, sigh, the stains on the ceiling. For the past twenty minutes I've been relating every detail about Marv and our date last night. I tell her about the Viagra pills. "Out of the thirty-two pills issued, there were eleven left."

"Did you want to stay?" she asks softly.

"Do you mean did I want sex with him? The answer is yes. Until I counted the Viagra pills."

"So you denied yourself because of your imagined drama about what Marv is doing? Anny, he has a life before you. Just as you have a life before him. He takes Viagra and you wrote about him. Instead of asking him if he's seeing anyone, you left. So he wouldn't know you on any level."

"Okay, already. Do I have to go over this psychobabble again and again? The man is right out of central casting, a poster boy for Viagra. Thinks with his cock. A perfect character."

"You don't want to see the real Marv. You just want him to use for your column?"

"I want it all. He makes me breathless—something in him evokes a deep passion in me that I've never let loose, even for my ex. But I always thought sex means love and commitment." I pause. "I was turned on by him, but when I discovered that he was taking Viagra, obviously with someone else, or many women, I backed off."

"So he takes Viagra. You don't know what his life is. You wrote about him, and he doesn't know what your life is. He's been wounded twice. You've been wounded. Yet you want everything from him."

"I want a *real* relationship. Not just sex."

"What do you mean by a *real* relationship?" she asks, after a long silence.

"You know, committed. He loves me. I love him. Not like my ex, who was busy fucking Conchita in the laundry room."

"You mean you want a relationship as in your fiction?" She sighs. "I'm just pointing out that you want a guarantee, but I wonder, if you had it all, if you would want it?"

"Well, it's not like I want him to give me more kids. Or even a dog. I want to be sure of whatever relationship I'm in—share a life, New Year's Eve, whisper in the dark. Anyway, boomer dating is a whole different game now that we're too old to think about a nice long future."

"Love is how you love yourself, Anny. It's about loving yourself. Then you could make stronger choices for yourself. You're afraid of rejection."

I watch the light float on the ceiling, then break into colored dots. "Well, you know my patterns with men. If they're too nice, I pull away. If they're elusive like my father, I move close. I'm a mess. I'm like one of those broken dolls you glue back together," I continue after a long silence. "It's fine as long as it sits on a fucking satin pillow."

She sighs. I can hear her shifting position, which means it's near the end of our session.

"Anyway, the men in this Viagra generation only care about sex. He's so into himself he didn't even read my column. Never mentioned it."

"Do you want him to read the Mr. X column?" Dr. Indira asks.

I shrug. As usual, she threw me for a loop. Do I want him to see that I have the upper hand, to show him that he's not that smart? Am I that defensive?"

"You're afraid, Anny." She sighs again. "Think about what Anny wants, instead of what you don't want, and you'll be happier within yourself. To do this you have to take risks sometimes and let your defenses down."

Silence. I hear the click of the light, which means the next patient has arrived. A door shuts. I inhale the sweet scent of the gardenias Dr. Indira always floats in a large orange bowl of water. She's right. To find contentment within myself is my quest, what I've been working toward, I think, reaching for a piece of Kleenex. She makes me realize that I'm not there yet.

"In my dreams, I can't fly," I say. "I'm a paper butterfly with wrinkled wings, schlumped on an old leaf. I want to fly out of the dream, but I can't move."

"Unfortunately, we have to stop."

I get up, blinking away the dots in front of my eyes and smoothing my hair, which is sticking up. Dr. Indira stands, and I look directly into her face. About my age, her long, braided silver hair is striking against her dark, smooth skin. A red dot is between her dark, soulful eyes. She is small, no more than five feet. She wears a yellow sari and a large amber ring.

"See you same time on Thursday," she says.

At the door I fumble with the damn lock, turning it to the right, then to the left, afraid I'm going to do it wrong while she stands there watching, and I'm wondering why she locks us up, as if I were a nutcase.

• • •

Outside, I blink several times, blinking away the light. I walk along Van Ness Avenue, the buses, sirens, heavy traffic, bicycles jarring me into reality. I pass restaurants and auto shops, then a homeless woman in a doorway, her blanket and worldly possessions neatly arranged in a cart. I drop some money in her hand, and when she smiles, her teeth are missing. I feel sad. I realize how fortunate I am, telling myself to stop whining about small things.

As I walk along Van Ness, admiring the sapphire color of the sky, I'm thinking about the session. Yes, Dr. Indira is right. I wanted to have sex with Marv, but I was afraid to take a risk because of my fear of rejection. So I didn't, but, God, how I wanted to.

I walk faster, passing city hall, the fading light shining on the gold dome like strips of gold foil.

I cross the intersection to Broadway, wanting to get home before it turns completely dark. Passing St. Brigid's Church, I stop and notice the bouquets of flowers dropped on the church steps, the scent of incense sifting from the open doors. Soon it will be night, when dogs howl, lovers meet, and the moon plays havoc.

When I get home, I work on a painting of a woman wearing a black hat and spindly, ankle-strap shoes, her nude body sitting inside a tall box. While I work, I remember that when I was married, I was always in my studio, painting. I ponder on what Dr. Indira had said about loving yourself, then I think back on my marriage. There was little communication, especially after Emily was born. Donald was furious, as he never wanted children. I had tricked him by not taking my birth control pill.

After a while, when I'm not sure where I want to go with the painting, I put away my tools and paints and get ready for bed. I water the plants and prepare the coffee for the morning. When the phone rings, I think it's Janet or Lisa, since they always call about eleven. Without looking at the number, I answer the phone.

"Hello, Valentine, it's Marv. Did I wake you?"

"Oh—no. Not at all. I'm painting." I clutch the phone.

"How have you been?"

"Busy with my work. And you?"

He tells me that he's excited about a twenty-carat, canary-yellow diamond he's going to look at in Milan. "It's perfect. A lot of dealers are bidding."

"Wow."

Silence.

"Can you see me tomorrow night? I thought we'd have dinner, then go dancing? You said you love dancing."

"Well, tomorrow is bad. Friday is the only day I have."

"Friday it is. Pick you up at seven."

"Great."

"Sweet dreams," he says.

I hang up. *Did that really just happen? Am I dreaming?* I feel like a young girl, the butterflies in my stomach swirling, giggling out loud. I spend the next hour in my closet, trying on shoes, shawls, deciding what I'll wear. I hate shopping, but I love taking my old clothes and remaking them.

The phone rings. It's Janet and Lisa.

"He called," I happily announce.

"Who? God?" Lisa asks.

"Marv," I reply.

"I knew he would," Janet says.

"Friday night we're going to dinner and dancing."

"Be careful with this one, sweetie," Lisa says in a cautious tone. "I just don't want you getting your heart broken."

"Lisa, relax!" Janet shrieks. "Honey, don't wear your highest heels. All you need to do is fall flat on your face—"

"Tomorrow, let's have lunch," I say. "I need your advice. Because guess what? I'm going to have sex with him."

Chapter 11

The next day, I'm having lunch with Janet and Lisa at the Waterbar, a happening restaurant in the Embarcadero. The windows are forty feet high looking out at the ships and the ocean and the bridge. Huge tropical fish swim in tall glass pillars surrounding the tables. It's a chic crowd, the men wearing black and the women wearing tiny corporate suits and designer shoes with spike heels and red soles. Handsome waiters glide about the room as if they're ice-skating. Our waiter, Jeremy, takes our orders, then brings our lemon martinis.

It's Janet's day off and she's decked out in a bright red, off-the-shoulder sweater, her hair high on her head. Lisa wears a chic black, short dress with silver jewelry and Manolo Blahnik, high-heel shoes.

"So for the first time in almost fourteen years I'm going to have sex. God, I'm a wreck. What if I don't know what to do?"

"Just close your eyes and pretend you're riding that bicycle," Lisa advises.

"Honey, all you need is a vagina," Janet says. "These boomer slickos will fuck a dog. Not to worry. You'll be off and running."

"But it's up to the woman. The mature woman knows her body, knows what to ask for," Lisa says, daintily sipping her drink.

"Fuck that," Janet snaps, her face all red. "You sound like one of those New Agey therapists who give advice on the G-spot. You don't ask. You seduce!"

"I agree," I say, laughing. "Anyway, women are more developed emotionally than men."

"Sure. Just ask Marsha Blumenthal. She gets Botox in her vagina," Janet says.

"I still smell a rat," Lisa says, choosing to ignore Janet's comment. "If Anny has sex too soon, poof, it's over. They need to know each other first."

"What's to know?" Janet says, her face turning red. "Haven't you heard? The boomer vagina is no longer in demand! We could be dead soon. You're living in the past."

"Well, I'm going for it," I say.

"Be sure your you-know-what isn't dry," Janet advises. "I E*Clip* vitamin E capsules into my vagina. The capsule gives off estrogen and keeps it moist. Only thing is, last time it got stuck in me and I had to go to the gyno to have her pull it out."

"Sex isn't everything," Lisa says. "John can't take Viagra, so he can't do it. He takes Coumadin. But we cuddle at night. He makes me happy."

"Happy *schmappy*. Not for me," Janet says. "I want the whole schmear."

"I'm nervous," I say. "Plus, when I lift my legs, my knees make clicking sounds."

"Don't be on top," Janet advises. "Your neck and boobs will hang. Be on the bottom, keep your head back. This helps the boobs and the neck."

"Well, be careful. This guy sounds like he's with someone," Lisa warns again.

"Anyway, I need more Mr. X stories, don't I?"

"Besides, the after-sixty men aren't long for the world," Janet says. "The last one I was with took so much Viagra his Life Alert bracelet went off, and the medics came. They gave me dirty looks and carried him out on a stretcher. And it was still hard, sticking up to heaven."

We laugh.

"I still dream Rhett Butler will find me," I say.

"Rhett is probably on Viagra," Lisa says, laughing.

"But he's too old to walk the stairs," I say.

"Okay, girls," Lisa says, gesturing to the waiter for the check. "We're taking Anny to Victoria's Secret."

"I'm fine," I protest. "I don't need to buy lingerie."

"You're not fine, honey," Janet says. "You can't wear your Walgreens special *shmatte* cotton underwear."

"Ditto," Lisa says. "Let's go."

An hour later we're at Victoria's Secret. I feel as though I've stepped into another world. Bras, panties all colors like candy, and nightwear are displayed like jewelry. Lisa and Janet are oohing and aahing over a black bikini panty so sheer, if I breathe on it, it will float.

"Oh, no. I'm too heavy for those. I have a sack starting around my stomach."

"Honey, forget the sack. When they're worked up, they don't notice anything."

Lisa holds up a black lace teddy with matching bikini panties and several wire bras.

"I don't need bras. I don't want to look like a Playboy Bunny."

"Fat chance," Janet says, peering at my breasts. "*Oy.* Your breasts hang like a nursing mother." Lisa agrees. They call the salesgirl, Mindy, who is no more than seventeen. She is willowy with a flat chest and ballet body.

Mindy looks me up and down. "Let me bring in some bras."

Before I know it, I'm in a dressing room trying on see-through, wire, lace bras. I choose one simple black lace bra. The girls come in, wrinkling their noses.

"Up! You need the straps tighter. Look at my breasts," Janet says, sticking out her chest. "See how they stick out?"

Finally, feeling gross, I purchase black lace panties that fit snug at the hip, a short, black, sheer nightgown, and a black lace bra.

"What if he doesn't invite me to stay over? Or I decide not to?"

"Honey, you make the rules. Do that right away."

"Set boundaries."

"I prefer sleeping in my frog nightgown," I say.

"Anny, no frogs for this guy," Lisa says.

"Be sure to use glide."

"Glide what?"

"It's pussy cream," Janet says.

Lisa winces. "Get a Brazilian wax. My girl, Svetlana, will do it."

"*Oy,*" Janet says. "She probably doesn't have enough hair left for a Brazilian. Go au naturel—he won't even notice."

"Oh my God. It's just a date," I say.

"It's not just a date," Janet tells me with a knowing look. "It's time for a whole new you."

Chapter 12

t's almost time. In one more hour, Marv will be here. I'm soaking in a gardenia bubble bath, shaving my legs and watching the clumps of dark hair floating in the water like threads, horrified by my age spots and the thin blue veins sprinkled along my pale legs. I close my eyes, remembering the last time I had sex—over fourteen years ago with my ex. He had been drunk, and as usual it was over in one minute.

After the bath, I study my naked body in the mirror, dismayed to see a slight fold around my waist. Even walking two miles a day hasn't helped. I spray Chanel perfume in the air and spin in it, letting the perfume settle into my damp skin. Then I put on the black lace panties, then the black lace bra. The new lingerie is hot. When I squint my eyes, I see myself at thirty-five—slender, the same long hair, long legs, and a flush of excitement on my pale skin—the anticipation of sex.

Next, I slide the black, sheer pantyhose over my legs, making sure there isn't a wrinkle. Then I slip on the black cocktail dress. It's silk, has long sleeves and a scooped, off-the-shoulder neckline. I put on my strappy, black high-heel sandals. Last, I wear my usual silver rings, and dangly silver earrings to my shoulders.

My cell phone rings. It's Emily. "Mom, have a good time tonight. Remember, be unavailable."

"But I'm available," I say.

"Harry says you should not be available."

"Harry doesn't know everything. He's been single for fifty years."

"Then don't ask us," she says. "We're busy people."

"I agree with Emily," Harry says from the other extension.

They sigh. "Call us in the morning."

In my black clutch purse I make sure there are keys, contact lens case, mints, condoms, taxi money. Just in case.

Five more minutes. My heart is beating so fast I feel as if it were going to pop through my skin. My cell phone rings. It's Marv. "I'm parked in front," he says in his smooth voice.

"Be right down," I say in my calmest voice.

"Take your time."

I hurry down the steps, praying that my contact lenses stay put and don't float around the way they sometimes do.

There he is, standing by his black Mercedes convertible, holding the passenger door open. He's wearing a long black overcoat and a black scarf, and in the dark his silver hair glows.

"Hello, Anny," he softly says. He kisses me on each cheek. "Are you ready to start the rest of your life?"

Wow. Is this really happening? I get into the car and he drives into the night.

Dinner is fabulous. We eat pasta and prawns and make goo-goo eyes at each other. Shamelessly, I'm flirting, lowering my voice, my hand pushing the wave back from my eyes. I'm crazed. What are we talking about? Who knows? Who cares? I'm floating on a magic carpet.

After dinner we go to the Sir Francis Drake Hotel, and holding hands, we ride this glass elevator to the top. I close my eyes, clutching his hand. I'm riding to heaven. All that matters is the night, nothing else. I feel electrified.

At the top, the room is something—all glass, looking out at Union Square. This orchestra is playing sexy love songs. Couples dressed in their Friday-night finest are slow dancing, strobe lights following them like bubbles.

After we're seated, Marv leads me to the dance floor. We dance to "Autumn Leaves." My arms are right around his neck, and I'm pressing my body so close to his body that we're almost one. He kisses me, and our lips are locked, and I'm lost in romance. Plus he's a terrific dancer, real smooth, his hand firmly on my back, doing these fancy crossover steps, dipping me low, then up again. Wow. We dance every dance, kissing and dipping, until the music stops for a break.

At our table, Marv orders a Frangelico, a nice after-dinner Italian cordial with hazelnut. Between kisses and sips from our drinks, Marv tells me that he's going to buy an apartment in Assisi. "We'll go there, Anny." He kisses me on the lips.

"I was there once, when I was eighteen," I happily say. "I remember the Leaning Tower of Pisa."

"Maybe in the spring. I want to spend more time with you, Anny."

Then he starts the *we* thing, telling me that *we're* going to go to India, climb Kilimanjaro, swim the Bay, and I'm enthralled. I'm kissing him, my hand stroking his thighs, not caring that people are looking. I can't keep my hands off him.

"The dancing was fun," I say, my face close to his.

"I love dancing with you," he says, then kisses me again.

"Me too. I mean with you." I laugh.

"I love everything about you, Anny. I want to be with you."

"How do you know?"

"I know. Do you want to be with me?"

"I'm scared."

"Of what? I won't hurt you."

"Of myself."

"Let's go to my place," he says.

"I thought you'd never ask."

Thirty minutes later, we're in Marv's bedroom. Except for the moonlight, Marv's bedroom is pitch-dark. Marv lights a candle on his nightstand, and immediately the pungent smell of incense, like burning wood, floats into the air. He presses a button and, wham, this Indian music plays. Now he's sliding off his clothes, kicking them aside. God, he's something. No protruding belly, long, slightly bowed legs, not an ounce of fat. "Please, don't look," I say, my voice faint. "I'm . . . shy." I slip off my dress, sneaking glances at Marv's firm, naked body.

Holding in my stomach, I pause so Marv can see my beautiful, new underwear, then I drop the panties and bra to the floor. He stands near the candlelight, looking at me.

"You have beautiful breasts," he says reverently.

"I'm nervous. It's been a long time since I—" Covering my breasts with my arms, I hurry into bed, trying to appear graceful and calm. His sheets feel like silk, not nubby or balled up like mine. I lie here, not knowing what to do. I'm afraid to move; if I move, my knees make creaking sounds. Then Honey jumps on Marv's pillow. To top that, she's glaring at me as if I'm an impostor.

"The music is nice," I say after awhile. "I've always wanted to go to India."

"We'll go," he says, his hand stroking my thigh.

"It's been a long time since I . . . I'm a little shy. It's been a long time—"

"That's all right. I'm shy too. Your skin feels like satin—like I knew it would feel—"

"Ow—wait—you're pressing on my leg too hard. Oh my God, my toe. My hammer toe. My God!" Of all times, my stupid toe sticks straight up and I'm in agony. I jump up and hop around the room like a nut until it settles down. "I'm so sorry—my toe cramps up—"

"It's fine," he says in an assuring tone. "Don't be embarrassed. It happens to me sometimes too."

I get back into bed and he gently kisses me and slowly moves on top of me, holding me tight.

"Be careful—"

"Better?" he says, moving his leg away.

"Better," I say, kissing him again.

"I love when you lick my neck like that," he sighs.

"It's Honey licking your neck."

We laugh. He kisses me then, at first lightly, gently, and I'm on fire. I don't remember ever feeling like this. The Indian music is rising, and we're kissing, really kissing, and it's magical, has a life of its own, and there is no age. No time.

Now my legs are wrapped around his broad back, and I'm whispering that I can't wait. "Do it now," I say, thinking, I hope it hasn't closed up from lack of use. But quickly, gently, expertly, he's inside me, and he feels perfect, like heaven. He's whispering that he's wanted to do this since he first met me, and I'm whispering that I feel the same. All reservations are gone, fears that I'll let out bodily noises and that my toe will cramp again. I can't get close enough. "Closer," I whisper.

"This is the best sex I've ever had with any woman," he whispers.

"Me too," I whisper, wondering whom he's comparing me to.

"You drive me crazy," he says.

I hold him tighter. This is magic.

"I could make love to you all night," he whispers into my mouth.

"Do, then."

"I've thought of nothing else. I imagined this." He kisses me passionately. "You're beautiful, so beautiful, Anny, your face, body, everything about you."

I lose myself in his arms as we whisper our fantasies, not wanting to part. At first I pull back a little, afraid to let go, like holding on to a ledge real tight, like not wanting to look down, afraid to let go and not wanting him to know that I'm falling, falling, like falling off a ledge, our bodies moving as if we're dancing, and he's holding me tight, so tight, and then he's moaning and my body is trembling and on fire like hot pins going through my legs, and then it's over. It's over.

We lie still, not parting, our mouths together. My hair is damp and my legs are still wrapped around his back. My body feels weak. Except for the sound of Honey licking

Marv's face, it's dead quiet. We kiss one more time and slowly he rolls off me.

"Do you want some water?" he asks after a long silence.

"No, thanks." I cuddle next to him. "I've never had an—orgasm so quickly. That was amazing."

"That was great." He pulls the coverlet over us. "You *are* a hottie." He puffs up the pillows, yawning and sighing. "Do you want to sleep with the soft or hard pillow?"

"Marv—if you don't mind, maybe I should go home. I have to get up very early." I wait for him to protest.

"Whatever you want, Valentine." He blows out the candle, and a stream of smoke drifts into the now cold, pale air. "I'll get dressed." He hurries into his dressing room.

So here I am, crawling on the floor, searching for my underwear, disappointed that he didn't beg me to stay, and wondering why I don't stay overnight, then assuring myself that I don't feel ready yet. I find my panties and bra and quickly stand, my knees creaking. I have to pee, but I'll wait until I get home. I'm shy about using his bathroom. The thought of his hearing me pee makes me cringe.

Shivering, I dress quickly, stuffing my bra into my purse and buttoning my jacket. I try to comb my hair, but it's a mass of tangled curls, so I smooth it with my hand.

"Are you ready, Valentine?" Marv asks, coming into the room. Wearing black sweats and a Giants cap, he's looking all nifty and awake, while my hair is sticking up and my face is all red and mottled. I fight the urge to rush into his arms, confess that he's Mr. X, that I want only to be with him, but then I tell myself now is not the time.

"Do you have everything?" he asks.

"Yes."

With Honey in his arms, we go down the elevator, to the garage. We drive into the night. Everything has changed. Never have I felt so alive, so full of desire. And the stars are still blinking. Really magnificent.

When I close the door of my apartment, I rush inside, and I don't turn on the lights. I slip off my clothes, letting them drop to the floor, then I go into the bathroom and turn on the lights.

This time when I stand in front of the mirror, looking at my naked body, my body looks different. My breasts seen fuller, the nipples still hard. Tiny bruises like welts, where Marv had caressed me, are patterned along my breasts, thighs, neck. I move closer to the mirror, looking into my eyes, trying to see the part of me that came out tonight. My eyes are brighter, and shining, and I'm smiling, as if I just won an award. It's a miracle. Good sex has nothing to do with age. For sure. Here I am, sixty-five-year-old Anny, afraid to cross intersections, and tonight I was all over him like a cat clawing a tree. It's as if he turned me upside down and all the sex came out.

I turn off the light and get into bed. Giggling like a teenager, I huddle under the blankets, imagining Marv's mouth on mine, and I slip into sleep.

Chapter 13

Later that morning, I feel ill. When I try to pee, I'm in agony. I schedule an appointment at noon with my gynecologist, Dr. Clay. Until then, I'm stuck sitting on the john, doubled over and trying to pee, so I call Emily to pass the time. I rave to her what a great night I had. "It was so romantic. We danced at the top of the Sir Francis Drake. He was so—attentive."

"Keep it going, Mom. Just don't sleep with him. Harry and I don't want you to get hurt."

"Of course not."

"Which means *of course you did*," she snaps. "Why else would you have a sudden bladder infection? You have cystitis. Like a teenager."

Silence. We're both waiting for the other to say something.

But I can't hold it in any longer—I burst out laughing. "Like a teenager? God, I hope not."

Emily is less than amused and sighs. "So did Mr. Wonderful ask you out for Valentine's Day? Has he called today?" she demands. I can hear Fred barking in the background.

"Not yet!" I snap. "I have to go."

"Of course you do. Because you know I'm right."

I lie down on the couch. I turn on the radio to the classical station, Pavarotti's magnificent voice filling my room, filling my senses. I'm listening for Marv to call, and as the morning progresses, I start to feel more and more disappointed. I had imagined that once we had sex, we'd be inseparable, making dates, on the phone. Looks as if age hasn't made me any less naïve.

Past noon, I arrive at Dr. Clay's waiting room. A nurse leads me to the bathroom for a urine sample. "Leave the bottle on the counter."

"Sure."

"Then go to the waiting room. I'll come get you soon."

I sit in the reception room, pretending to look through the outdated *New Yorker*, observing the pregnant women sitting across from me. They look so content, I think, remembering when I was pregnant. We lived in Happy Valley, in a dramatic five-thousand-square-foot house on several acres. I hated suburban living, schlepping around the pool in my rubber thongs—smoking and yakking with my pregnant friends about Jell-O molds and carpet samples.

The door opens. "Anny Applebaum," the nurse calls. She holds a chart and wears a pale blue cardigan sweater with tiny pearl buttons. I hurry past the pregnant girls and follow the nurse down the narrow hallway to the examining room.

"Everything off," says the nurse. "You know the drill."

She closes the door, and I undress quickly, squishing my panties and bra into my tote bag. I put on the lousy blue paper gown, tying it in front. I sit on the edge of the table, my legs dangling over the edge, shivering.

In walks Dr. Clay. He's a great doctor, and he's known me since Emily's birth. He looks a bit like Sidney Poitier.

"Hi," I say, always shy at the doctor's office.

"I'll examine you. Scoot down." While he examines me I stare at the spot on the ceiling, my eyes closed. I count to ten.

"You can sit up now, Anny. You have cystitis, a nasty bladder infection. Amoxicillin will cure it. He pauses, looking at me intently. "Don't have sex for at least a week. Also, I'll write you an extra prescription, and before you have sex next time, take two."

"Uh-huh," I say, embarrassed that he knows I had sex.

He stifles a smile. "Anny, I advertise in the *San Francisco Times,* and recently I read the Viagra Diaries."

"Wow. I'm pleased."

He chuckles. "I like Mr. X."

"Glad you like it," I manage to say.

"Anyone you know?"

I nod. I turn red. "Not really."

He looks at me the way a parent looks at a child who is telling a lie, then says, "And next time, treat sex like a fine wine. Don't drink it all at once."

I'm blushing.

He pats me on the shoulder. "Anny, sex will keep you young. Enjoy."

Near evening, after taking the antibiotics, I'm feeling better. But I'm restless and upset that Marv hasn't called. I had imagined that after such a great night, by now he'd send flowers, ardently make plans to see me again.

I sit by the window, looking out at the pathetic shrinking moon, obsessing over why Marv hasn't called. Maybe he had an emergency diamond sale. Or meeting. He seemed to always be going to meetings, and on quick business trips. Or am I obsessing because I'm so insecure? Here I am sixty-five, suffering from a bladder infection, and I'm replaying Marv's every word, gesture, kiss, knowing that he's elusive. But I realize that the more elusive he is, the more I want him, and I feel the same kind of passion for him that I felt at seventeen with Seymour Alterman, my first love, making out in the backseat of his car, my merry-widow bra off and doing everything but.

I turn on the television. I watch a Barbara Walters special

on aging and people living to 150. All these great-looking people over a hundred, not even wearing eyeglasses, sitting in nursing homes and reminiscing. God, it's something. Age is so irrelevant; some people at seventy are like thirty, and some at thirty are like seventy. But I can't concentrate. I feel sexually charged. I feel inspired, a bundle of energy.

Quickly, my heart beating fast, I lay out my brushes and palette, turn up the Billie Holiday tapes, and slide the eight-foot canvas that Ryan had helped me stretch years ago and lean it along the wall. Feeling exhilarated, as if some muse has taken over, I begin working.

With a thin stick of charcoal, I quickly draw a naked woman lying along the bottom of the canvas, her shapely legs provocatively raised and ready for sex. Her face is turned slightly to the viewer, and her hair is flowing behind her. I work faster now, shading the woman's skin a pale flesh color, darker around the nipples. I work for hours, blending white with the flesh color, smudging the paint until it has a blurry effect, like a dream. Satisfied with the figure, I paint elongated high heels on her feet, and then a black, flirtatious hat, tilted slightly on her head, and finally, a dab of red as her luscious mouth.

When the music stops, I keep working, not stopping to edit, to fix, but to let the woman emote her sensuality, to let everything loose—alive. With broad brushstrokes, I paint the sea behind her, a mist of mauve, the sand white as chalk. Finally, I apply a wash of distilled white paint over the painting, letting the wash pour over the woman so that she recedes into the mist, her glowing, pale body open and seductive.

On impulse, I remove my work shirt and press my naked breasts into the wet paint, pressing until my imprint is secure. Now I'm firmly inside the canvas. Stuck there forever.

It's time to stop. I stand back and realize that my hands are shaking. I can't stop looking at the painting, as if a part of me became her. Unlike my ladies in boxes, caught and scratching to emerge whole, here the strokes are wild and loose and the woman is free. I feel as though I were just reborn, or something. I'll call her Natasha. I always imagined that my muse would be called Natasha.

After I clean my brushes and put away my paints, I pour gardenia bubble oil into a tub of hot water. I light scented, pink candles around the old-fashioned, white tub. I submerge my body into the hot water, enjoying the candlelight making wobbly shadows along the pale ivory walls, the steam clouding my face.

Washing the paint from my body, I wonder if Marv is sleeping, if he's thinking about me. Will he call soon? Of course he will, I assure myself. After all, if I'm feeling this, then he is. Next time I'm sure we'll be inseparable.

Later then, before I go to bed, I call Janet and Lisa and we make plans to have lunch on Monday at Macy's cafeteria. "I have lots to tell you," I say.

Finally, I sleep.

• • •

Monday at noon, I'm at lunch with Janet and Lisa. Janet is on her lunch hour, and wearing her dark blue Chanel uniform, a blousy top with short sleeves, and pants. Her recently dyed flaming-orange hair is piled high in coils on her head, and her dark, emotional eyes are artfully made up and shadowed in gray. Lisa is picking at a Cobb salad, elegant in a Versace, royal-blue, long-sleeve dress with a slit up the side, and a silver, arty, rectangular pin. Her regular facials and Botox make her skin taut and so smooth you can almost see through it.

"So tell. You look like you swallowed a canary," Janet says, leaning forward, curiosity on her intelligent face.

"You're glowing," Lisa says wistfully.

I tell them about the night with Marv, how utterly fantastic the sex was, how I loved being with him, and that he made me feel like a desirable woman, a way I'd never felt. "We made love for six hours," I continue, feeling almost breathless. "So not only do my legs ache from being stretched around his neck all night, but I got a bladder infection and had to go to Dr. Clay and take antibiotics. Still, the sex was great. Out of the ballpark."

"Now you have him pussy-whipped," Janet says. She takes a bite from her tuna melt. "When he calls next time, say you're busy. Hold out for longer weekends."

"After these men get great sex," Lisa says, "they put you away like a library card. Then they go to the next."

"On top or bottom?" Janet wants to know.

"All ways," I reply, flushing. "Only my hammer toe kept acting up. Not to mention I was worried I'd—well, smell down there."

"Honey, they don't give a rat's ass if you smell. They love the you-know-what. I told you, spray some Chanel No.5 on it."

"He's fabulous," I gush. "Only thing is, after this great sex, on the way home he was kind of—distant, like, 'Anny who?' No, 'I'll call you.' Or, 'What about tomorrow?' He just wished me luck on my writing. I think he's shy—overwhelmed by our passion or something."

"Shy my ass," Janet says, popping a french fry into her small mouth. "It's memory loss. These boomer guys don't remember anything from one vagina to the next. You're lucky. A lot of these boomer guys—one grunt and it's over."

"You're telling me," Lisa says. "They're not interested in the L-word. I don't want sex without love. It doesn't work."

"I agree," I say.

"Honey, maybe you can just take him for what he is—a great lay. At our age we can have sex without love. Don't listen to Lisa. No matter how women's roles grow, if she's over sixty, honey, she's a throwaway."

"Well, I don't believe this," I say. "I can't wait till the next time I'm with Marv. When I'm with him, making love, I'm in my youth. There is no age."

"Don't count on it," Lisa warns. "After sixty the party is

over. Unless you want to wear his dead wife's clothes, drive her car, and sleep in her bed."

I hear my phone beeping, and frantically I dig it out of my huge red leather tote bag. "Oh my God," I say, looking at my smartphone. "It's Marv. He e-mailed me. Oh my God. He writes, 'Hey, Valentine, I miss you already. Kisses, Marv.'"

"Valentine? What the crap is that?" Janet makes another funny face.

"Because he says I remind him of Valentine's Day, martinis, and old movies."

"Definitely, I smell a rat," Lisa says, grimacing.

"Don't sextext back," Janet advises.

"Excuse me, I'll be right back," I announce. "Bladder time."

I go into the ladies' room. Once I'm in the stall, I e-mail Marv. *I miss you too. I send kisses right back at you. I'm on fire. Your Valentine.*

I remove my jacket, pushing my black, low-cut sweater off the shoulder, and snap a picture of myself with the phone. Oh, God, here I am in a bathroom stall, posing like an old pinup girl, smiling like a harlot. I'm hooked. I send it to Marv.

Back at the table, I try to avoid Janet's stare.

"Well, it's time to go," I say, applying red lipstick to my lips.

"Well, good luck with Marv," Lisa says. "But be careful."

Janet snaps, "Anny is lucky. Let her enjoy. Most of these men can't do a thing."

We say good-bye, promising to call later.

We go our separate ways, and I walk in the sunlight, hurrying to the taxi stand. I walk with my coat open, slightly swaying my hips and not all huddled over the way I used to walk. The sun feels good on my face, and when a man smiles at me, I smile back. Everything is different now.

Chapter 14

Two weeks have passed and Marv hasn't called. This drives me up a wall. No matter how much I tell myself it doesn't matter, I'm devastated. But my work is going great. My last column, "He Doesn't Call After Sex," is a huge hit. My fans love Mr. X. And I don't care that I'm writing about him. "He uses me, I use him," I tell Dr. Indira. I keep interviewing more boomer guys for the column, but my fans are clamoring for Mr. X. I'm inundated with e-mails asking me to write about him again. They can't get enough of Mr. X. I'm asked to speak about boomer dating to a large group of boomers, called Boomers in the Know. I accept and prepare index cards with my notes for my talk the following day, titled "Everything Is Possible After Sixty."

•   •   •

The next day, at midafternoon, I arrive at the Hilton Hotel. I'm wearing black pants, a violet cashmere cape-style top, and my new leather ankle boots with violet shoelaces.

A lovely silver-haired woman greets me. "I'm Marci Finklestein, event coordinator." She is short, stocky, and wears a pale gray silk dress with ropes of pearls. Her eyes are blue. "Over a hundred people signed up. We love the column."

"I'm so glad."

"Mr. X is so dreamy, but—elusive. He's a bad-boy boomer. Do you actually know him?"

"You'll have to keep reading," I say, avoiding her question.

We shoot the breeze, and she tells me about her Mr. X. "He's a nut. I've been with him for four years. He's sixty-eight and thinks he's twenty-eight. The man has had two knee replacements, can hardly walk." She lowers her voice. "He's an animal in the sack."

"Uh-huh."

"With their knee and hip replacements, they still think they're hot. It's the damn Viagra."

"Is it Viagra?" I say. "Or that we're new women in a new generation? With new values? Where age doesn't matter? Women fight age too, you know. They get fake boobs, hair extensions, and Botox, and the men get Viagra. Everyone is trying to be younger."

She looks reflective. "Good point. Well, save this for your talk."

She leads me into the conference room. People are seated, some in walkers. They wear Velcro name tags. Many of the women look militant, smarty types wearing hiking boots and shawls, and others with partners. The room is huge and smells like nylon and Naugahyde. The carpet is light blue with red flowers in it.

On a wood podium sits a plastic water pitcher and a dusty glass. The lights dim and Marci Finklestein introduces me. She holds up my column "Breakup." She goes on about how my columns touched a nerve. "Anny Applebaum believes that everything is possible after sixty, and does she need Mr. X? Let's give it up for Anny Applebaum."

Wild applause as I adjust the mike to my mouth. "Hey. I'm sixty-five and I want to be a movie star!"

Applause. Stomping.

I feel energized. I don't look at the notes I made on small index cards. I wing it, telling them about my life and struggle with ageism. "At thirty when I was married and a mom, and living in the suburbs, I dreamed of becoming a novelist. But my husband and my family said that I should forget writing and stay home and give dinner parties! At forty, I was told that I was too old to go back to college. At fifty, I was told to buy a burial plot, and at sixty, and divorced, I was told to get a real estate license and a new husband. Hey. I want it all, fame, fortune, and undying romantic love!" I shout into the mike, my voice echoing. "I want to change the world. I don't want Botox. I want me!"

They go crazy. Some of the men are whistling.

"So know that everything is possible! Write your books, get those gardens going. Don't listen to the ancient fallacies that after sixty we're supposed to only play bingo and meet a man. That's not the only thing."

Wild applause. I love this. I feel inspired. I feel new.

Then it's over. Marci announces a buffet of cheese and wine and that I will be happy to answer any questions. She leads me to a table in the back, where a crowd has formed a line. I sit at this table, nibbling on a piece of blue cheese and a grape. All these men and women are asking me about Mr. X, the men challenging me about Viagra.

"Nothing against Viagra," I say to a tiny man with a narrow head. He's about seventy, and pale and nervous. "I think it's the best thing since the cure of polio. This is not about Viagra. It's about attitude. Most boomer-plus men want to date women no more than thirty."

"So why not?" says a stocky, fit man wearing a black running suit. A snake is tattooed along his muscular arm. He has gray, thin hair and a pin-shaped head, and tiny, nasty eyes. "I'm fit. I'm a marathon runner. I'm seventy-one and I run with thirty-year-old Russian girls. I had a bone-density test and my doc says that I have great bones."

"Bones, yes, they're important," I say, sipping coffee now.

"No offense, lady, but the last woman I made love to at your age, her bones cracked. Most women your age are shrinking, have humps in their backs, knee replacements, cancer, the whole bit." He cracks his knuckles.

The day winds down. I exchange cards with many women and men. All want to be in touch, to be part of a group. I feel moved. I love talking with the boomer women, trying to inspire them to pursue their dreams.

I hurry outside to meet Emily. She's meeting Harry later in the city and we agreed she'd pick me up and bring me home.

Later that night I'm at the computer, polishing "Boomer Bad Boy," when the phone rings. Right away I see Marv's number on the screen, and my heart goes wham-bam. I answer on the third ring, sounding breathless, as if I just found the phone or something. "Hello—"

"Hello, Valentine," Marv says in his smooth voice.

"Hello." My heart's beating so fast I'm afraid he can hear it.

"How's my stranger?"

"You're the stranger," I say, trying not to sound irritated. "It's been awhile. So how have you been?"

"Great. I would have called earlier but my son and I, his wife and my granddaughter, spent the past weeks in Bolinas, at my vacation home."

"Sounds wonderful," I say, thinking he came home early to see me.

"We had a great time. My granddaughter's so gorgeous."

"Sounds good."

"I miss you, Valentine."

"Uh-huh."

"Do you want to do something Saturday night?"

I hesitate, wondering if I should play hard to get, but reminding myself that he is asking for a Saturday night, that I need material, and that maybe I should give us a chance. Plus I'm dying to see him. "Well, yes, Saturday is fine," I say in a low voice, not wanting to sound too eager.

"Dinner?"

"That will be lovely."

"Bring an overnight bag. I want you to spend the night."

Chapter 15

t's Saturday night and I'm on the phone with Janet. "Should I wear the Victoria Secret nightie or the cotton T-shirt?"

"It won't make any difference, honey. They go for the vagina. They don't hear, they don't see, they only want one thing."

"Anyway, he invited me to stay overnight. It's a first."

"Good for you! Make sure you're not a groggy mess in the morning. These boomer guys want the hair floating on the pillow, the pretty, smiling princess in the morning. They want what they didn't get when they were younger, with their divorced or dead wives."

"Call me Monday. Ciao."

I pack an overnight bag with three underwear changes, and two outfits, imagining that we'll spend Sunday together, and my best perfume. I finish dressing, decking out in the new H&M red sweater that slides off one shoulder, and my new black pants. Finally I put on my red platform shoes with the five-inch heels. I'm ready.

When he calls, I rush downstairs, my heart beating fast, and we drive to the restaurant. "You look gorgeous, Anny," he says.

We're at the restaurant, drinking vodka martinis with three green olives. I'm feeling like a bride on a honeymoon. Marv is being attentive, ordering all these fancy appetizers—smoked salmon, caviar puffs, potato puffs. He's wearing a silver turtleneck, cashmere sweater the same color as his hair, and a hot-looking, beautifully tailored tweed jacket.

We chat about our lives, restaurants we've been to. We don't mention our last time together nor do I ask why he became so distant. Worse comes to worst, I'm getting material, I assure myself.

After our second drink he starts chatting up a storm about this rare pink diamond worth a million dollars a carat. "It's perfect," he says with a wistful sigh. "Like you, Anny."

"I'm not perfect."

He clicks his glass on mine. "I can't wait to make love to you. You're all I thought about. I'm through with the dating scene."

"Why?" I ask, hoping he'll say because of me.

"The younger women don't want to meet a seventy-year-old man, and they don't have the intellect you have. You're different." He finishes his drink. "I have the best sex with you that I've ever had with any woman," he says, sounding as if he got the right answer on a quiz show.

"But I want a relationship," I blurt, watching his face for a reaction. "I don't want casual, date sex. I want—love."

He looks at me dead on, his appraising eyes reflecting nothing. "I'm not having sex with anyone but you."

After an awkward silence, he opens the menu. "How about dessert?"

"I love strawberries."

"I bought some for our breakfast tomorrow."

"This is my first overnight since my—husband."

"Well, you came to the right place." He blows me a kiss.

An hour later, we're in Marv's bedroom, undressing wordlessly. Quickly, we hop into bed and hold each other tight. God, I'm climbing all over him like a cheap suit, dying for him. Before I can breathe, he's on top of me and we're going at it, and this time there isn't any fumbling or self-consciousness, just this passion, and I'm pressing my body to his, inhaling his scent, and enjoying the feel of his satin skin. "I love this. I couldn't wait to be with you," I whisper.

"I just look at you and I want to fuck you," Marv whispers, pressing deeply into me. "You see it in my eyes."

"Don't you dare move. Stay like this forever," I whisper.

And so we make love for hours, until our bodies are drenched, until our lips are raw; magic, orgasmic sex. I dismiss all of my questions about him, and I'm in love.

After it's over, I press him tight in me. We stay deeply inside each other until it's near dawn—I can tell because streams of gray light make stripes along the dark. Tonight, I reached a point of sexual intimacy that I've never had, even with my husband. I'm trembling, knowing that Marv took me to a place that I can never forget, and I'm clutching to him. My body is full of him.

"Let's get some sleep," he says, his fingers gently brushing a strand of damp hair from my forehead. "I'll close the drapes, and I bought a fan. You said you couldn't sleep without a fan or Excedrin PM. I bought both."

"So you knew I'd be here."

"You had to. Just as I had to be with you."

Eagerly, like a young boy trying to please, he gets up and turns on the fan. He bring me a glass of water with two Excedrin PM. "Take these," he says, his face relaxed into caring. "You need your rest. You work too hard."

I swallow the pills and then settle into the mound of pillows. For a while, we lie still, preparing ourselves for the intimacy of sleeping together. "Is your fan all right?" he asks.

"Perfect."

"It's like a fucking hurricane in here," he says, yawning.

I laugh. I snuggle closer to him. "I dream that I fly. Do you dream?"

"I float in a shallows, the current takes me. I float forever and I never age." He yawns. "Good night, darling." He kisses me lightly on the lips.

He turns then, and in a minute there's only the sound of his and Honey's snoring. I try to sleep, but I'm afraid if I fall asleep, the night will go away, and I want to remember everything. So I lie here, frozen into the dark, afraid to breathe. I watch Marv sleep, the slight flutter of his eyelids, the light on the mound of gray hairs on his chest, the high and wide forehead, a head like a beautiful sculpture, the sleek skin.

I sleep too. I dream that Marv and I lie in a garden of blooming pink roses, making love.

I watch morning flood into the sky, obliterating the night. I glance at my watch. It's a little past seven. I have to pee, but I don't want to get up first. I don't want him to see how red and mottled my skin gets after sleeping. So I lie still, wishing I were home in my apartment, going through my morning rituals and playing back every detail of the night.

"Are you awake?" Marv asks, yawning. Honey is next to him, licking his face.

"How are you this morning?" I say, my hand covering my mouth so he won't smell my morning breath.

When the phone rings, he has a frozen expression on his face until the ringing stops. After a tense pause, he glances at his watch. "It's my son calling. I'm supposed to see my granddaughter today. I always see them on Sunday mornings."

"Oh, sure," I say, wondering why he didn't tell me before. Wondering if it's really Debra who called.

"Do you want to take a shower with me?" he politely asks. "I have a new showerhead. It has three thousand holes. I'll soap you up."

"No. I'll shower at home," I say, waiting for him to say that I'm not going home, that I'm spending the day with him, but he says nothing.

He glances about the room. "Make sure you have your earrings. Don't forget anything, Anny." He looks under the bed, then in the sheets, acting as if God forbid I should leave something behind.

I want to shout, *Hey! I'm here. It's Anny Applebaum. Remember? The woman you fucked all night? Promised a trip to India? Why are you worried I'll leave something behind?*

"Here's your watch," he says, holding up a thin gold one, its face covered with diamonds. "Don't forget it."

"I'm wearing my watch."

He frowns, as if trying to figure it all out, then drops the watch in a drawer in the nightstand next to the bed. Scoops up Honey and walks into his bathroom.

I listen until the sound of the shower starts, to his voice

as he sings "Lady Is a Tramp," before tiptoeing over to the nightstand and sliding open the drawer, ever so slowly. I carefully pick up the watch, admiring the glitter of the diamonds encrusted on its face, and turn it over in my hand. Is this Debra's watch? But if it were her watch, he would know it and not show it to me. So whose watch is it? Or was he trying to tell me that he has someone else?

Carrying my clothes and feeling disappointed, I hurry into the guest bathroom. So he won't hear me pee, I turn on the faucet, hoping I'm not making too much noise, thinking it's so odd that Marv acted as if he didn't know anything about the watch. Or did he? Or am I imagining that after he received the phone call he turned cold, and what happened to all the emotions from last night? Now I'm angry that he is dismissing me on a Sunday, plus I noticed that he took his cell phone into the bathroom with him. He's probably calling his ex-wife, or am I imagining all of this? Maybe I'm looking for obstacles so I can avoid intimacy? Or am I angry because I know deep down that Marv exists in moments and that at any time he will disappear?

I dress quickly, wearing my new jeans and black turtleneck sweater that I had bought for this weekend. *Be careful. Make sure. Play your cards right.* Until I have evidence that he's seeing his ex-wife, I'm not going to leave him. I'm going to wait and see what happens.

I rinse my face with cold water, brush my teeth. After I brush my hair into a twist at the neck, I stuff my things into my overnight bag. I zip it up, and assuring myself that every-thing is going to be fine, I open the door.

"Breakfast is almost ready," he says. He's in the kitchen, and I stand in the doorway a minute, watching him at his deluxe, bright red espresso maker, making coffee and carefully drop-ping thin lemon rinds into tiny glass cups. Toast pops from his jiffy, deluxe toaster. He's in his own world now, away from the world we were in last night, and again I'm feeling like a guest that he is hurrying out. As I stand here watching him, I want to hug him, to make some kind of intimate contact. Instead, I chat about how I like espresso and the different kinds of coffee machines, but he doesn't answer. He's folding linen napkins into squares.

I notice a sculpture I hadn't seen before. It's a wonder-ful cubist face of a woman with bright red lips. "I like your sculpture. Is it new?"

He doesn't look up. "My decorator and I bought it at an auction. The sculpture's name is *Alice*. Isn't she wonderful? She looks like real art."

"What does real art look like?" I ask sarcastically.

"Museum quality. Expensive."

"Uh-huh."

"Now, let's eat, Anny. You like egg-white omelets and sourdough toast?"

"Perfect." I sit next to him, thinking he's well dressed for a morning with his granddaughter. He's wearing an ice-blue cashmere sweater and a cashmere tweed jacket over snug jeans.

The table is set with orchids and beige linen place mats and napkins. He spreads jam on his toast, careful not to go to the edge, then neatly eats his cheese omelet, never spilling a crumb or a drop of egg. He eats as if the omelet were the most important thing of the day, sighing and repeating, "I make a great omelet."

"Your orchids are so beautiful. I love orchids," I say, trying to make conversation, wondering if he feels as shy, as tense, as I do.

"My ex-wife Debra and I raised orchids. Now they're part of the divorce. We share them."

"Uh-huh. I see." I wonder what else they still share. I'm nibbling on the toast, trying not to chew too loudly, telling myself to hang in, that maybe he's not a morning person, that I'm only imagining that he's cold.

"I'm leaving for Palm Springs on Thursday," Marv suddenly announces, not looking up. "I'll be gone about three weeks. There's a diamond show."

"Oh, I see." I try to keep my voice up, wondering whom he's going with.

"I have a small place there," he quickly continues, averting his eyes. "I bought the house years ago so Debra could play tournaments. She's a tennis pro, and after the divorce I use the house—"

"So you've told me," I interrupt. "Anyway, I have a dead-line tomorrow. I have to finish writing my column on sixty-plus commitment phobes."

"What does that mean?" He holds his fork suspended in the air.

"It means men who only want sex and no relationship. Emotional morons who always want a more perfect woman. Younger. Prettier. Rich. They can't sustain emotions."

"Sounds interesting, Anny," he says, a deadpan expression on his face.

"Anyway, I guess you don't read my columns." A part of me wants him to know that he's material and that I don't buy into everything about him.

"Oh, I have. They're very good," he says, avoiding eye contact.

"Odd that you don't know whose watch that is."

He looks me dead in the eye. "I think it's my decorator's watch. She was here last week moving furniture around with her assistant, and she might have left it there."

"I see." I feel relieved, reminding myself that I'm always looking for the bad instead of the good.

Glancing at his watch as if I were not there, he gets up and clears the table, brushing the tiny crumbs into a metal bin, murmuring that his cleaning woman will be in soon and that he can't stand disorder. One more time he sponges the marble counters, complaining out loud, as if to no one, that his cleaning girl hasn't done a good job lately. "I like order," he repeats. Then, as if remembering I'm here, he looks at me. "Are you ready?"

"Sure."

It's a little past 8:00 a.m. Marv drives fast, a distracted expression on his face, and bratty Honey is lying on his lap, looking smug. A low, pink fog floats over the half-dark sky. The streets are empty and cold. Soon they'll be crowded with couples enjoying their Sunday. Here I am, going home, dropped off by my lover. Dismissed again. For sure, he and his ex-wife sound more like husband and wife. Or am I imagining this? Dr. Indira says I tend to imagine the worst. Then again, not everyone is like me. Just because Emily's father and I haven't spoken since the divorce doesn't mean that divorced people can't be friends.

When we finally get to my apartment, he keeps the motor running and the seat belt on, as if he's ready to go, and there's this awful silence, as if he knows I'm waiting for him to make plans to see me, to say something, anything.

"Well, it was . . . great," I slowly say.

He kisses me, his lips pursed into a dry wrinkled kiss. "Good luck on your writing," he says formally.

I fight the impulse to say, *Hey, mister! Is this a blow-off? What do you mean "good luck," and when am I going to see you?* But I say nothing. Instead, I jump out of the car and hurry into the building.

The rest of that day is a nightmare. I feel a mixture of ecstasy and gloom. One minute I hate Marv, the next I'm assuring myself that I'm just overreacting to the watch episode and looking for reasons to end our relationship.

After I bathe and unpack my overnight case, I try to write. But I can't write. I need to process what went wrong. I feel once again rejected, and I wonder, is Marv really this indifferent, or has he read my columns and is trying to keep his distance? Or does he not care that I'm writing about him? Whatever, he's impenetrable, and it drives me crazy. Still groggy from not sleeping the night before, I make coffee, then Emily calls.

"Why are you home?" she demands.

"Why are you calling?"

"Home on a Sunday? I thought you were going to be with him on the weekend."

"I had work to do," I lie.

"Why didn't he spend Sunday with you? Men his age don't drop lovers home on a Sunday morning."

"Emily, please don't check up on me."

"Harry agrees the signs aren't good."

"What signs? We hardly know each other."

"You know each other well enough to be fucking like rabbits."

"Emily. Please don't talk like that. I'm on the edge and this certainly isn't helping."

"You sound upset. I worry about you."

"I'm not upset," I insist.

"Was it good?"

"Emily, I'm not talking about my sex life with you."

"Of course not," she says, clearly exasperated. "Because that's all you do with him."

"You don't know him. In many ways, he's wonderful."

"He's an in-the-moment guy. What about a real relationship?

"In time."

"Time, my ass."

"He's just afraid. He's been wounded."

"He gives you nothing," Emily rants. "Has he ever given you a flower, a box of candy—anything? And don't mention those gardenias again. He's insulting."

"He's wounded. A big lion licking his wounds."

"Not too wounded to have sex with you all night. Harry says he's a serial JDater junkie."

"It's more than that!" I shout. "He's more than that. Trust me, or I wouldn't be with him."

"Sure you would. You'll do anything for a column. Face it. You're using him to write about. And you're pretending you're writing about someone else. Your Mr. X has a tiny white dog, drives a black Mercedes, and is a diamond dealer. You're in love with Mr. X and you're playing a dangerous game."

"Stop it. You don't know him!" I shout. "He's more than that. Trust me, or I wouldn't be with him."

After I hang up, I think about Emily's saying that she and Harry checked JDate. She's right. At my stage, why am I dropped off on a Sunday morning? Now I'm upset. I turn on the radio to the classical station. Pavarotti's magnificent voice fills my room, filling my senses. No matter how much I assure myself that Marv and I are just getting to know each other, I know this isn't true, know that he doesn't sustain emotions, that after sex, we're like strangers. But Marv said he was through with JDate. Maybe I'm imagining that I'm more than a sexual diversion?

I quickly turn on my computer and check the site. Sure enough, he was on JDate an hour after he took me home. Once again I'm stunned. I feel exploited. All along I was right. Right that he was on the prowl for the next woman. Little does he know that Mr. X is bringing my column recognition, but even though I still feel guilty about exploiting him, I assure myself that this is my career and that I'll turn Mr. X into a winning situation for my career, plus have great sex. An even exchange. The game is on.

Furious, I decide to write "Don't Forget Your Watch," my next Mr. X column about sexual encounter, its expectations, and about how he turns off afterward.

I write about the dinner, every word, the dancing.

Like heaven, we were immersed in desire.

In the dark he glows, his eyes like an owl's, his touches tender and passionate, but when the fire goes out, and in the light of day, he's cold, distant.

Does sex mean love? Mr. X makes love like a hungry boy—affectionate, daring, eager, tender, all those things—but after, he goes to another place, a place I can't reach, like I no longer exist.

What about men who don't call after sex? Is there something deeply wrong with them, or is there someone else? Or is it different after sixty? Are my expectations unrealistic? I want intimacy, more than just sex.

For the next two hours, I take careful and detailed notes about our night together. I write, *I notice the candle—burned down more since the last time I was there—the tin box of mints with painted roses on its top on his nightstand. The red silk pillows on the chaise in the bedroom weren't there the last time. His decorator? Also, the orchids; always there're fresh orchids. His ex-wife raises orchids.*

I don't stop writing until I'm exhausted. I close the computer. As always after writing, I feel as if I were waking up from a dream—as if I were in another place. I straighten up the apartment, water my plants, stack the *New Yorker* magazines, and arrange my baskets of dried leaves and shells along the wood table next to the wall. A mouse appears from behind my bookcase and scurries into a corner crack. Poor mouse. I want to catch it and let it go outside. It's trapped.

After dinner, restlessly, I work on some sketches, drawing women wearing hats. I remember Marv driving to the restaurant last night, when he stopped the car to look at the mansions along Broadway, a wistful expression in his eyes. "Now that's what I call a home," he said.

What about his other women? Is it his ex-wife? It's what he doesn't say or do that is his real self, is Mr. X. His words don't mean anything: His silence, the way his eyes appraise me when he thinks I'm not looking, his sudden affection when he wants sex. But then I remind myself that I'm capable of denial, of living inside the fantasy and believing it's real. So am I kidding myself? Is Marv like me, fearful of falling in love?

Restless, and feeling anxious, I call Janet and tell her about the night with Marv.

"Was it great?" she asks, chewing. She's always eating.

"Yes, but he turned cold afterward again. Plus there was a gold watch on his nightstand and he thought it was mine."

"Short interest span, honey. These men are emotionally retarded. You're lucky if these oldies can remember your name. Feel lucky he can get it up. Honey, enjoy. Gotta watch a rerun of *Mad Men*. We'll talk tomorrow."

Nine days pass. Marv still hasn't called, but the watch piece is a hit. The column is going wild, and I'm asked to be on Boomer Talk Radio the next night. It's a popular call-in, late talk-radio show that emphasizes boomer issues. I accept. I can't wait to talk about the Viagra generation and Mr. X.

The next day, near midnight, I'm at the radio station, which is on the fourth floor of a tall building on Montgomery Street, in the heart of the financial district. I wait in the greenroom, a small, dusty room with a glass partition facing the radio host, a squashy, tired-looking woman wearing earphones.

Waiting with me is a disgruntled man in his late sixties. He introduces himself and tells me that he's written an important book on how to get rich. "Thirty-five years out of Harvard, and here I am on this schlock show."

"Shame," I murmur.

"I'm an important author." He wears a Giants cap on his balding head. His lips are thin. "My publisher puts me up in fleabag hotels. Dreck. I'm leaving them. They'll be sorry."

The door opens. It's his turn to go on his three-minute segment.

I flip through an outdated *People* magazine.

I listen to the speakers on the wall. The disgruntled man talks about himself, and no one calls in.

The door opens and he exits, slamming the door behind him.

"Rachel Applebaum," the host calls.

"Anny," I correct, entering the small glass booth. I put on the headphones.

A copy of my last column, "Leave the Lights On, Please," is open on her desk. About forty-five or so, she has a pretty face. She wears huge, ratted hair, and her nails are polished blue. She lights a cigarette, slowly exhaling smoke. "This boomer gig is the shits. All the old guys are hitting on me. The young ones can't compete with four-hour erections."

"Well, there's more to it than that."

She finishes eating chili between taking drags from her cigarette, complaining about the "lousy industry." "I'm not paid enough to sit here all night and interview a bunch of freaks."

"Well, I'm sure it will bring you somewhere."

She jabs out her cigarette, instructs me not to say a word until she raises her arm, then she begins the countdown.

She introduces me as "Rachel Applebaum, of The Viagra Diaries."

"Anny," I correct again.

"Rachel Applebaum will help you be young," she continues. She yaps about aging for at least three minutes, how really yucky it is in this society, that Rachel Applebaum has a new slant on it. "She's pushing eighty and has the key to the fountain of youth. She even believes in sex for the older woman."

"I don't believe in the term *older*," I say. "Sex is sex at any age. It's based on desire, spirit, not age." Then the volume of call-ins is huge. Most of them sound drunk. They yell that I'm a "bitch" and that I don't know what I'm talking about. "Do you know, lady, what it's like to wear diapers, to be lonely?" Some sound vulnerable, alone in the night, alone in themselves.

"Viva Viagra!" shouts a man, then he hangs up.

"Hey, lady! Meet me after the show. I'll show you what Viagra is!"

"Mr. X is a fucking sex freak!" says a woman with a New Orleans accent.

Angry women call in, yelling that they read my column and that Mr. X is only interested in "young," and that I should dump him. Others tell me that they are saving money for face-lifts, have lost their jobs over a wrinkle.

"It's attitude," I say. "Your youth never left you. It's in you. Find it."

"Mr. X is a shit!" shouts another woman, ranting that I need a "real man."

"And that was Rachel Applebaum, ladies and gentleman," interrupts the host. "Thanks, and good night."

As if I'm not there, the host resumes eating her chili. I hurry outside.

Market Street is shockingly quiet after midnight. Iron gates are in front of the stores, and the windows are dark. I walk along the dark, almost empty streets, feeling suddenly lonely, until I see a taxi, and I rush toward it, yelling, "Hey, mister! Don't you dare leave. Wait!"

Almost tripping on my high heels, I hurry into the taxi.

Several days later, on a Monday evening, Marv calls and tells me that Palm Springs was hot and he worked hard, selling a diamond to a rock star from England. When I hear the sound of his voice, I feel as if I were going to float off into space again.

THE VIAGRA DIARIES

"Do you want to go to dinner tomorrow night? Or tonight?" he says, lowering his voice.

I hesitate. "Well, I have a deadline—"

"Anny, I want to see you. Anny, I miss you."

"Well, tomorrow then, but it has to be an early evening."

"I'll pick you up. I'll order in. We'll watch the next episode of *Mad Men*."

The rest of the day, just thinking about him, I feel conflicted about writing about him, even loving him, and I decide to keep Marv separate from work. Then instead of going on my usual walk, I get my hair washed and blown. Also, I get a manicure and a pedicure, with dark crimson polish.

I'm ready to let my fears of rejection go and embark on my new journey. I'm ready to take a risk.

Chapter 16

"Whose dog is this?" I ask the next night at Marv's co-op.

"It's Coco, Honey's mate," Marv explains. "She's Debra's dog. In our divorce agreement she kept Coco and I kept Honey. When one of us is away, we often take care of each other's dog."

"How sweet." I feel jealous.

"Don't be that way. Debra and I are just friends."

While Marv makes cocktails, looking all hot in a chocolate-brown sweater and snug jeans, I excuse myself, and in his bathroom I once again open the medicine cabinet and look at the bottle of Viagra pills. This bottle contains more pills than usual and it's hard to tell how many he's taken.

An hour later, we're in his bed. We make love as if time hasn't passed between us. He's passionate, whispering that I'm all he's thought about, that I'm the best sex he's ever had, and that I'm the one. I forget all my doubts, and making love with him brings me to another place. It's wonderful.

Afterward, he gets up and brings two glasses of water on a tray, places it on the nightstand, then settles into the bed, clutching his remote. He pushes a button and the mattress goes up. "Isn't this Tempur-Pedic mattress wonderful? It's foam and good for the spine. It keeps me young."

"Great," I say.

We're sitting up and eating take-out shrimp chow mein and green beans and watching *Mad Men*, which I adore. I love the stylized black and white, the sixties clothes, remembering that's how I used to dress. Thank God women's roles have changed and we have more choices. After the episode, I chat about how great my column is doing, tantalizing him to ask about it, but he merely nods and says, "Good for you."

The show is over. Marv clicks to *David Letterman*. He fluffs the pillows behind our heads.

"Are you sure you don't want anything?" he asks again.

"Just you."

He doesn't answer. I'd hoped that sexual intimacy would sustain into something else. Instead, he's engrossed in Letterman's interview of Kim Kardashian, who is whining that fame is really hard, and it's hard to follow her heart. I want to say, *Hello, I'm here. Where are you? Hello, I'm Anny. Remember? The woman you just fucked?*

When the show is over, he clicks off the television, the static making a buzzing sound.

"I can't stay tonight. I think I have to get home," I say after a while.

"Anny, please, honey. I'll make breakfast in the morning."

"Well, I have a column to write—"

"Anny, stay." He pauses, looking hurt. "I know you think I'm with someone else, but I'm not. Only you, Anny. You have to trust me."

"I have work to do," I say.

"I want you here with me," he says.

"Well, I have to leave early in the morning," I say, pleased that he persisted in asking me to stay.

I cuddle next to him, then he clicks the remote off and it's dark. We kiss, and he turns to his side, Honey and Coco on the soft pillow. I try to sleep.

The next morning I wake, slowly opening my eyes, and I'm surprised to see that Marv isn't in bed. I hear the water running from his dressing room. I smooth my hair, and feeling disoriented and slightly groggy, wearing Marv's black silk pajamas, I hurry into his dressing room. Marv is standing naked at his double sink, rinsing his face. "Good morning," I say, kissing him.

"Good morning, darling."

"I overslept. You wore me out." I laugh.

"Look, Anny, I got you a toothbrush. Just don't squeeze the toothpaste from the bottom. See, Anny? From the top, then fold the bottom."

"Sure."

He kisses me on the mouth. "It was a great night," he whispers. "Put that into your column. They'll never believe it. Most men my age are wearing leisure suits and looking at porn."

"You're a tiger," I say teasingly.

I love the new intimacy of brushing our teeth together. So different from when I was married to Donald. He would gargle, then make these moose calls, then spit into the sink. Then rush to work without looking at me. Intimacy is something I've never had, never learned, and I'm feeling all warm and glowy.

Standing next to Marv, the light full on our faces, I brush my teeth, careful not to splatter the sink or make gargling noises. Everything he does is elegant, precise—even brushing his teeth. He uses his superduper electric toothbrush, then rinses his mouth with peppermint mouthwash, releasing the wash softly, so elegantly. He opens a plastic container with the days of the weeks marked on each tiny compartment, removes some pills, drinks water from a shiny glass, swallows, then washes his hands. He slips on his underwear.

As I watch him standing in his black, Calvin Klein underpants—slim, tanned, combing his thinning hair—see the loose skin on the back of his legs, the pink of his scalp through his slick, sleek, carefully combed hair, the slight tremble of his hands, I feel a wave of overwhelming love. I put my arms around his waist and hold him tight, inhaling the soapy scent of his smooth skin, almost swooning.

He kisses me on the lips, his mouth cold and full of peppermint.

"I'm crazy about you," he says, holding me tight. "I love being like this with you."

"Wouldn't it be wonderful, Marv, if we were like this all the time?" I watch his handsome face in the morning light.

He kisses the top of my head. "Anny, you're very emotional. You just *think* you'd want this all the time; trust me, you wouldn't. Enjoy the moment. We're old now. I don't know how long I'm going to be here. It's inevitable. One of us will get ill, and we'd have to take care of each other. So enjoy the moment."

"I want more than moments," I blurt, watching his stoic face for a reaction.

He nods, a tense expression on his face. "I've already done it the other way. I've been divorced twice." He resumes dressing.

I finish dressing, trying not to show how hurt I feel. I slip on my jeans with the painted flowers and my long, black, off-the-shoulder cashmere sweater.

On the drive to my apartment, Marv is quiet, distracted, as if his mind is in another place, as if we hadn't spent all night and the morning together. The Frank Sinatra CD is on high, and a tight expression is on his face, as if he's holding in something he wants to say. Or that he's angry. Instead, he hums along to "My Funny Valentine." He stops the car in front of my apartment, the motor running. Marv kisses me lightly on the lips and thanks me for a "beautiful night."

"Please don't say I'm the best sex you ever had."

"Why not? You are," he says.

"Take care." I get out of the car, and before I get to the front door, he drives away.

I rush through the dim, heavy fog, past Ryan, who is watering the roses before he goes to work. He watches Marv drive away. I hurry into my apartment.

Marv disappears for a week and I continue to write my Mr. X columns. The last column, "You're the Best Sex I've Ever Had," is a hit. Women write in angrily reporting that they'd rather have love, and why does it have to be separated? Why can't he say "I love you"? they write. While he's gone, I swear off him, telling myself that he's only material and what do I need him for? But deep down I know this not to be true.

When he returns, we resume seeing each other. He calls on Mondays, invites me out for Tueday or Thursday, rarely on the weekend, explaining that he has gem shows to go to or some business thing. I bite my tongue, feeling guilty that I'm writing about him, and assuring myself that he loves me and just can't express it the way I want. Each time I see him, we resume our pattern, going to the North Beach Restaurant, high on our sexual attraction, and then back to his place, where we make an effort to watch a movie but never finish it. As usual, afterward he's cold, and I vow never to see him again. Hoping that he'll change, every day I go on JDate, and he's always logged on. Furious, I integrate my unspoken grievances into my next Mr. X column, enjoying the notoriety and recognition. Ironically he's the catalyst for my success. Not to mention the great sex.

But then just as I plan to tell him it's over, I'll be in the middle of working and suddenly I'm remembering the night we made love in his shower, the hot spray of water on us, our laughter as water filled our mouths. He lives in my skin.

At times I don't know whether it's Mr. X I love, or Marv. But I can't stop. My body craves him, and I fantasize that we're living in Paris together, and I'm writing and painting, and finishing my novel. Obsessing over Marv, I take constant notes. I find myself creating scenes. I wear my fuck-me, Joan Crawford ankle-strap shoes, a trench coat over nothing, and in the middle of the night I go to Marv's home and have fabulous sex. I keep us on the high and never predictable.

In deep now, assuring myself that my Mr. X columns are the key to success in my career, I take copious notes on what Marv eats, doesn't eat, his overly staged house and too neat couture, his buffed nails, his huge donations to the Jewish Federation, his obsessions. How he worries about a scratch on his polished car. But then he has this creative side, a penchant for beauty—his love of the sun, nature, beautiful things.

As with the Joan Mitchell, Picasso, and de Kooning paintings I love, which I look at for hours wondering what's underneath the surfaces, I want to dig out his soul and see what's there. Sometimes I catch him staring at me, an appraising look in his critical eyes, the same look I'd seen when he was looking at a diamond, turning it and holding it to the light, checking for flaws.

Chapter 17

A heat wave comes to San Francisco, but at night a veil of fog floats over the city like pink chiffon. I'm at my desk, working on "The Morning After," my next column about Mr. X. But lately, the more I've been seeing him, the more I have mixed feelings about writing about Marv. Sometimes I feel guilty about using him for material. But the column is gaining more recognition and I can't stop.

In the morning, Mr. X turns into a different person. Distant, and tense, he hurries through breakfast, then drives me home. I rush to the door and watch Mr. X drive off in his black Mercedes. As he disappears into the traffic, I wonder if I'll ever see him again. Something was off, very off, especially when his cell phone rang all night and he retreated into another room. . . . Or am I the one who retreats behind my imaginary wall when I feel vulnerable?

I write until shadows sprawl along the walls and daylight is fading. I turn off the computer and turn on the small, milk-glass lamp on my white cement table. I read the draft of the column and then ponder my list of new interviews, sorting out e-mails, trying to decide what my next column will be. The radio is on the classical station. Alisa Weilerstein is playing the cello, Dvořák's Cello Concerto in B Minor. I love the cello. It sounds like the soul.

As far back as I can remember, when I'd hear my grandmother play the cello and accompany my mother at the piano, I'd tremble with excitement.

There's a knock on the door.

I open the odor and am surprised to see Ryan. He holds a bouquet of lavender roses. "Hello," I say. He's wearing black boots and a wrinkled, slightly dusty black shirt, and his unruly hair sticks up. A Leica camera dangles from a strap around his neck.

"Hey, Anny. I was worried about you." He looks anxious. "What's going on?"

"Nothing, really."

"I thought you might like these roses," he says shyly. He looks down at his shoes and seems nervous. "They're from my garden in Sebastopol. They're Sterling roses."

"I love them." I inhale their scent. "Come in."

He hesitates. "Maybe for a minute." He holds a book about Kissinger under his arm. He's always reading about foreign affairs. Regularly, he attends lectures at the World

Affairs Council. He stands close to the painting leaning along the wall. I fill the tall glass vase with water and arrange the beautiful roses. I put the vase on the glass table in front of the window, enjoying the light on the petals, turning them silver.

I watch Ryan intently study my painting *Natasha*, his face close to the canvas. He stands quietly, but I can feel his restless energy. When he looks at art, he comes alive. He moves close to the painting, then back again. He doesn't say anything, but I can often read his silences and understand what he doesn't say. So different from Marv, who uses silences to hide his feelings. They're as different as day and night, yet when I think about Marv, I feel that spinning feeling I'd have as a young girl when yearning for something unapproachable.

"I like that your women are coming out of the boxes, Anny. Something interesting is happening. She's sensual."

I smile. "Do you think so?"

He squints his eyes and moves closer to the painting. "The woman has the same playful, come-hither look in her eyes as you do."

"You see me that way?"

He glances at his watch. He pauses. "I have to get going soon. I have—"

"A date?"

"My friend Nina and I are photographing jazz clubs tonight."

"I made fresh coffee," I finally say. "Stay for a moment."

For a while, we sit on the sofa, drinking our coffee. He tells me about his latest assignment with *National Geographic* about war victims in Vietnam. Looking sad, Ryan tells me that when he was seventeen his father, an ex-marine, kicked him out of the house. "Because I didn't want to join the Marines."

I remain quiet. I'm aware of the sudden shift of his tone, of the pain in his eyes.

"So, Anny, I'll be going to Alaska next week with my two photographers. I'll be gone for several weeks."

"Sounds good."

"I'm photographing ice."

"Ice is interesting."

He smiles. We're sitting close to each other. My hand brushes his. "Are you still seeing Marv?"

"Not all the time. But, yes, I'm seeing him."

He shrugs. "Well, I have to get going, Anny." He takes his cup into the kitchen and rinses it.

At the door, he sweeps his hand along my cheek. Even in the darkening room, I can see the blue of his eyes. "Anny, someday I want to take you to see the monarch butterflies. I'll be photographing them for a nature series in *National Geographic*. They're beautiful."

"I'd love to go. I love to watch them fly—light pouring through their wings."

"They don't fly in the rain," he says.

He tells me about a place near Sebastopol where thousands of monarch butterflies are let loose. They only live about six months. "You can hold them, drench yourself in them. They can't fly in the rain, so I want to go soon."

"I love butterflies. To think that any creature so magnificent comes from a caterpillar—no wonder they can't live so long. They're too beautiful."

"Maybe beauty isn't supposed to last too long," Ryan reflects.

"Like love," I say.

"Yes, like love, Anny. Sometimes things are just too much to last long." He kisses me on the cheek. "I'll call you when I return from my shoot."

It's near midnight, when the day is past and the night is still. A time to reflect. For a while I sit on my favorite chair, listening to Latino love songs. The sensuous music fills my senses. Earlier I checked JDate and still Marv isn't on. What does this mean, that he's with someone and doesn't have time? These questions are driving me crazy, and I'm feeling disconcerted, and restless.

In my closet I open a box where I keep my childhood letters, stories, and journals. For a while, like searching for some clues to why I am the way I am, I read my journals. Then, just as I'm closing the box, on the bottom, I see the journal marked June of the year I met Donald. *We danced all night to*

"Moon River." I want to spend the rest of my life with him. He's a beautiful man. He's safe.

I close the box.

I undress for bed and then slide under the covers. A wind rattles the windows, and stars blink in the sky on and off, like my heart.

Chapter 18

Monica called and she wants to see me. The column has been going great guns, but she says we need to talk. Rarely does Monica want to see me. Usually I just fax my column, and that's it. Given the popularity of the column, I'm hoping I'll get a raise. God knows I can use it. I'm getting tired of buying bags of spaghetti and cheap toilet paper at the Discount Chinese Market.

I dress carefully in my one-and-only conservative black pantsuit and polish my black boots with the taps on the heels. I love the sound of the taps when I'm walking and imagine that I'm dancing with Fred Astaire.

I put on my dark glasses, grab the leather Coach briefcase that Emily gave me and my rubber raincoat, and call a taxi to take me to Monica's office on Market Street.

• • •

I arrive at the Starlight Building and take the old freight elevator to the second floor, to the *San Francisco Times*. I hurry along the narrow hallway past open cubicles with reporters and assistants on their cell phones, typing on their Apple laptops, engrossed in their work. Since Monica took over the paper, the *Times* has grown. I hurry along the narrow hallway that smells of Xerox machines and synthetic carpet into Monica's office.

Monica is on the phone with someone, leaning back in her leather swivel chair, twisting a strand of pale blond curly hair around her long, slim finger. She's small and stick-thin. She wears a bright red shawl around her shoulders, cigarette ash stuck to the wool. She talks with a slight lisp, and at the end of every sentence, her voice lilts up as if in question. She continues to whisper into the phone. Monica's desk is piled with papers, drafts, clips, empty cups, books, Dixie cups filled with paper clips, and thumbtacks. The Mr. X columns are pinned to a work wall behind her desk. She's talking with some writer, insisting on more research. "Don't bullshit me. You can do better than this," she says. Everything about her is smart. But it's her eyes that distinguish her—sharp, heavily hooded turquoise eyes.

She hangs up the phone, rubbing her temples and muttering that she's had it with "no-talent writers who think they know everything." I clear my throat and her had snaps up.

"Anny! Good to see you. Your columns are fabulous! *San Francisco Star,* eat your heart out." She lights a brown, thin cigarette and exhales a long stream of smoke. "I hope you don't mind if I smoke." Before waiting for my response, she slaps my most recent column, "Cum Loudly," on the desk. "*It* went through the roof. Your fans went crazy."

"Wow, that's funny."

"Except for the owner. Bunny wants more *issue*-oriented pieces."

"Issue-oriented? Isn't dating, and sex, an issue? Seniors do have sex."

"I know. But Bunny Silverman thinks pussy is a cat. Hey! I take orders from upstairs. Not to worry. Just keep writing the Mr. X columns. Keep going." She reads my list of titles, her finger tapping the page as she reads along. "I'll run 'You're the First Woman of Sixty-Five I'm Attracted To.' 'Jerk or Jerk Off.' 'Are Diamonds a Girl's Best Friend?'"

"Great."

"Sales are up, up, and I put in a request for a raise. You deserve it."

"Thanks, Monica. I can use it."

"Of course you can. Do you think the wealthy diamond dealer is going to give it to you? Hey. Been there. Done that."

I laugh.

"The watch piece hit a nerve," she continues. "You were great on the boomer call-in radio show. Wait till you read the blog—women from all over the country complaining about their Mr. X." She takes a drag from her cigarette. "I get what you're doing, Anny. My so-called ugly boyfriend, head of accounting, tells me that he doesn't believe in love. He believes in Viagra. And he's only forty-five. He complains that I have fat thighs, and this turns him off. You're right. Even ugly men are jerks."

That evening, thrilled about my raise, and even though Marv hasn't been on JDate for a while, I'm determined to write a new Mr. X column. "Does He Introduce You to His Kids?"

Mr. X talks about his son and granddaughter all the time— so far, he hasn't introduced me to his family or his friends. Is it because I just fit into a slot in his life—the sexpot slot? Or do I fill the role that his ex-wife took away? Is it that he thinks because he can pop those blue pills and get it up, all that matters is his pleasure? Am I compartmentalized?

When twilight covers the room, I stop writing. Tonight, I'm gong to read. Before I do, I pull the drapes, leave one window open for air, smooth the white, puffy cover on my bed, fluff the oversize pillows, then change the water in a vase of purple tulips.

The sound of traffic swishing through the rain is peaceful. Blue streaks of lightning zigzag along the dark sky like blue dreams.

I turn on my Janis Joplin tapes. I love her voice, her authentic passion, her fire and rage. I lie on the couch reading *Birthday Letters*, by Ted Hughes. The poems are about his marriage to Sylvia Plath. They are so moving, so full of passion, regrets, and sadness, that as I read, I cry. The poems reveal the author's great love for Plath, and their ending makes me sad and I'm feeling really low, sinking in this place of empty, gray terrain, wondering why great love has to stop. When my land phone rings, I answer it, and I'm surprised to hear Marv's voice.

"Do you want some company?" he asks, his voice seductive.

"Well . . . I'm reading. I—"

"I want to see you," he persists. "I miss you."

"Sure, come over," I say, pleased by his fervent tone. This is a good sign. He's never seen my apartment, and I can't help but feel as if this is the beginning of our sharing more things.

"I'll be there at nine," he says.

Ten minutes to nine, I run around, fluffing pillows, moving papers from my coffee table to the box underneath my desk. I want my apartment to look neat. I light candles, dim the track lights, then change into black leggings and a black, long-sleeve top, beaded with the word "freedom." I arrange the emerald satin pillows along the faded white couch, quickly vacuum the white, fuzzy rug mostly covering the hardwood floors, restack the array of *Artforum* magazines on the glass table.

When the doorbell rings, I hurry to the door. My heart is beating fast. I stand in the hallway, watching him holding Honey in his arms, hurrying up the stairs. His long trench coat is damp from the rain.

"I hope you don't mind," he says, kissing me. "Honey has been home all day alone."

"Sure," I say, forcing a smile. Honey glares at me.

He shuffles in, glancing at the half-finished canvases and charcoal drawings taped to the walls, the half-full jar of peanut butter with the spoon stuck in it, and an array of open books still on the chair. "This is cute. Very arty."

"The apartment is cluttered. Too many books."

He glances at the dangling boxes, and a seven-foot, half-finished painting leaning along the far wall. It is of a woman sitting on top of a box, and she is naked. She wears a black hat with a black veil over her face, and her legs are crossed as she gazes beyond. He then looks at *Natasha*, then he looks back at me, questions in his eyes, as if trying to see into me. "It's nice."

"She's Natasha. My alter ego."

"Why are the boxes—hanging?" he asks, looking unsure of himself.

"Because boxes aren't supposed to hang. I like to explore the opposite of the norm."

He shrugs, then sits on the edge of the couch—forward, as if he's not sure he's going to stay.

"I like Joplin," he says after a long moment.

"I missed seeing her in the sixties. I was living in the suburbs, giving dinner parties. I missed a lot. Especially the women's movement."

The music rises. Like teenagers after their first kiss, we both feel shy, self-conscious, strained. After all, we've only been together on his terms, on his turf, and in his bed.

"Your naked woman with the hat is—interesting. Why the hat? All your women in the paintings wear hats."

"They like hats."

"Like you."

"I don't wear hats when I'm naked."

"But you can."

"Next time I will."

He smiles. "This is a funky place. You really are unique, aren't you? What's with all those boxes on stands?"

"As I've told you, I make boxes. I hope to have a solo show of my paintings and boxes someday. My dealer, Inga, wants at least twenty paintings and more boxes. I have a lot to do. Plus, I have my column deadlines."

"Well, you keep busy."

I hate his patronizing tone. "I don't do it to keep busy. It's my work."

"I want you to hit it big. Then you can buy a nice house, get out of this apartment. The world would be yours." He smoothes a tiny crease on his sleeve, his large hand pressing it until it's gone.

"I don't want to own the world. I want to help the world.

Also, I like this apartment. Sorry I don't have a trust fund, a face-lift, and a doorman. I don't care about wealth the way you do."

He shrugs. "Don't be defensive. You know what I mean. I want the best for you."

"Unfortunately, I do know what you mean. You want me to be famous so you can show me off, then introduce me to your friends. If I were rich and famous and thinner, then you'd love me. Meanwhile, I'm sixty-five-year-old Anny, with a messy apartment and funny clothes."

"Oh, Anny. That's in your mind. I've never mentioned thin. I love your body."

I fight back the tears brimming in my eyes. "We see each other for dinner and an occasional movie. Then you disappear for weeks. Would you do that if I were some supermodel like all of your exes?"

"Do you have any vodka?" he asks after a tense silence.

"No, sorry," I snap. "And you don't need to go in the bathroom and take your Viagra because I'm not going to fuck you tonight. So if that's why you came over, forget it. I'm tired of feeling like I'm an appointment."

His eyes are now half-closed, arms stiff by his sides. He sighs. "I don't want to marry again."

"Whoop-de-do! Who said anything about marriage? What about a relationship? Is that so hard to ask?"

"I don't want to hurt you, Anny."

"You just did. Get out."

Then, after this awful silence, he jumps up. I watch him lift Honey to his chest, slip on his loafers, glance at his watch.

At the door, he kisses me lightly on the lips. "I'm leaving for Mexico for a gem show. I'll be gone for ten days. Good luck with your writing." He actually looks relieved more than anything else.

Holding Honey, he shuffles down the hall, his shoulders slumped forward, and hurries down the stairs. I stand in the doorway, his scent drifting behind him like a haze of smoke, fighting the impulse to rush after him and hold him close.

At the window I watch him slightly shuffling, get into his car, then drive away. I watch the stars slowly fade and slip into the dark, wondering: who is this man I write about? Obsess over? This serial dater, a man who obviously doesn't care enough for me? This man I fantasize about, who lives in my dreams so close I interpret his silences, feel his lips on mine, hear the shuffle of his walk, his sighs, his velvet voice. This man as juvenile as a fourteen-year-old boy—is shallow, glib, charming. This man I'm in love with.

Chapter 19

D r. Indira pulls the drapes closed.

I lie on the couch, and she waits.

"He acted like he was slumming when he came to my apartment," I finally say. "Oh so polite he is, but he ignores me, shrugs, and looks away when I mention my column. He only wants sex and takes the small part of me—what he wants. His indifference is abusive. Just like my ex-husband. God, here I am sixty-five and I haven't learned a thing."

I roll the Kleenex into a ball.

"I have what I want for now," I say, after a long silence.

"Because you're writing about him?"

"He's a good character. Anyway, as soon as I write about him, he's someone else," I say, feeling defensive.

"If you believe this, then you're paying a high price for a story."

I watch a fly float around the light, thinking that its wings look like glass. You can see the light through them.

"Sometimes I feel guilty that I write everything I know about Marv into Mr. X. But then I see him on JDate an hour after he's been with me and I don't feel so bad. No way does he have anything on me. But I think Marv might be a louse. Hey! 'Louses and Jerks,' that's my next article.'"

She waits.

"Also, even though he says he's not, I know he's with Debra. There are signs. The watch. Empty wine bottles in the kitchen—and she drinks wine. When his mind is on her, he drinks wine. Plus, the candle is burned down. Also, the K-Y tube was moved from his nightstand to his bathroom—"

"He's told you he isn't with anyone else."

"I don't believe him."

"You are writing about him. Maybe you should tell him the truth. How you really feel?"

"He'll leave."

"Or maybe he'll stay," she quietly says. "Or maybe you only want him the way it is—for material? For the game? If you write about him, you can keep him exactly as you want, and you don't have to do very much. Writing about him is a defense."

"Against what?"

"Reality."

"What do you mean 'reality'?"

"Find out the way things really are and not as you want them to be."

"I want long-term love. To be loved. To be with someone who wants love all the time, not just sometimes. I want love *and* sex, not just sex." I reach for a Kleenex. "He knows how I feel."

"Oh, no, he doesn't. You go out of your way to act like you don't care. Because you're afraid of rejection."

"Of course I am. Why not?"

"Do you think it's right that you write about him?" she challenges.

"Did Picasso need permission to paint his wives? Besides, once you interpret the person you're painting or writing about, he's no longer the same."

Her phone rings. I wait. I dare her not to answer. The room is stuffy, and Kleenex balls stick on my black cords.

"I want a full commitment. I love sex with Marv, but how can you have sex without love? I want to be with someone who loves me, cares about me, who wants love all the time and not just sometimes."

"Do you really?"

"Intellectually, I do."

"Like Ryan?"

I watch the shadows slide along the wall then break, which means the session is over. I sit up, dizzy from lying down so long. I sneak a glance at her, and then, trying not to lose my balance, I clunk to the door. I turn the lock twice, to the left, and the door opens.

That night, at home, I think about my therapy session. What a mess. I'm conflicted about this sex-love thing. Sure, I'm thrilled about the column, but I wonder if I truly loved Marv and he loved me, would I write about him? Sell him out the way I do? But still, Marv hasn't been on JDate for a while. This is a good sign.

I call Janet. I've been worried about her. Recently she had an emergency gallbladder surgery. She works so hard, and her health hasn't been great.

"What's up, honey?"

"The usual. He's away again. Stuck his nose up at my apartment. Plus, he hasn't said the L-word."

"Don't count on it. *L* is for 'lust.' After sixty the love party is over."

"But what about having only sex? I want more than just sex. How can you have sex without love—without emotional connection?"

"Very easy," she says. "I had great sex with a man for four years. Until he forgot my birthday."

"See? That's what I mean. It's the indifference that bothers me. Marv doesn't acknowledge anything else about me, except for the great sex. At least lately he hasn't been on JDate."

"Honey, unless you want to meet a widower, wear his

dead wife's clothes, drive her car, and sleep in her bed, this is what it is. Be glad you have passion. Look at poor Lisa. She's got a dude who's made for her on paper, but he has a thingy that couldn't fit in a keyhole. My pinkie finger could satisfy her more than he can."

"I don't want to be with a man who only wants sex with me and still shops around. I still want the dream—you know, 'I love you,' and he says, 'I love you too.' "

She sighs. "The last guy I said that to screamed that older Jewish women want it all, that we're never satisfied with an orgasm and a brisket. That's what's out there, honey. At least you and Marv have great sex and he cares about you. Get some sleep. Enjoy. Honey, I have to get my eight hours or I'm dead tomorrow. Love you."

"Love you too," I say.

The next day, a little past dawn, I awake with the worst pain in my neck. It really hurts. So does the top of my head. At first I think it's because I sit hunched over the computer all day, or maybe that I slept funny. But the pain gets worse, and now I can't move. I'm really scared. I'm not used to health problems. I always think that I'm going to stay the same, full of energy and doing what I do, into eternity. I do my positive visualizations, holding my crystal butterfly. It has powers. I assure myself that when I wake the next morning, my neck will be normal.

Only now I can't bend my head at all. I can't bend my head to dress. Sitting on the john, doing anything, is an ordeal. Panicked, I call Ryan, but I remember that he's in Sebastopol. Not wanting to bother Emily and Harry, in agony, I put on my trench coat over my nightgown, grab my wallet, and take a taxi to Mt. Zion Hospital. When I arrive at the emergency room, it's a nightmare. Patients are lying on gurneys, some moaning and yelling for a doctor. Finally, a tired-looking nurse sticks me on a gurney in the hallway, assuring me that a doctor will see me soon.

So six hours later, a young, pimple-faced intern wheels me to X-ray. All the way upstairs, he talks baby talk to me, telling me not to be scared, reassuring me that I'm in good hands. He wheels me into this dingy, smelly room. He has me stand against the cold tile wall, and he pushes my head back and forth until settling it into position. He runs to the X-ray machine, yelling for me to hold my breath. I'm in agony.

"Now, don't move!" he orders. "Hold your breath!"

I hold my breath, but when I do, my neck hurts, and I feel as if I were going to faint. My paper gown keeps opening in the back, and I can't breathe.

The intern wheels me back through the hallway. All the rooms are taken so the doctor leaves me on the gurney, advising me to "rest." I'm on my cell phone with Emily and Harry, who are on their way to San Francisco. Emily advises me to make sure my will is intact and that my life insurance payments are up-to-date. The doctor comes, and I hang up the phone.

He has a small face and a pear-shaped body. He holds up a huge X-ray of my neck. "It's degenerative arthritis," he says, sighing. He points to the white shadow, explaining that it's my deteriorating neck bones. "Soon your spine will collapse, and you'll be losing your balance." He gives me pain pills and writes a prescription for physical therapy. "If you don't get therapy, you'll be crippled forever."

Waiting for Emily and Harry, groggy and depressed, I watch an older man stand by his ill wife, holding her hand and talking softly to her. This is a moment when I want a mate, not just for the hot sex and candlelit dinners, but also to be with me in the bad moments, like now. To age together. I'm remembering a few weeks ago, when Marv had an epidural and I sent an anchovy pizza—his favorite—to his home. But when I told him on the phone about my colitis attack, he didn't call for days.

"There you are, Mom," coos Emily. She's wearing a red beret and jacket. Her dark, silky hair hangs to her waist. Harry holds my hand and tells me not to worry. Plenty of people my age have arthritis and lose their balance. "You'll have a walker," Emily says in a baby-talk tone. Harry agrees.

"Hey, I want to go home," I say. "I have no intention of losing my balance, having a walker, or playing bingo."

"Well, just don't lose your heart," Emily advises, looking at Harry, who looks away. I know they've been talking about me.

They lecture me about the pitfalls of aging, warning me to acknowledge my age and to be more "careful." Then they drive me home.

I'm drowsy. My neck rests in a thick, cumbersome brace. Emily fusses over me, makes sure that the brace is securely set, smoothing the blankets. I'm feeling depressed, helpless, imagining myself someday dependent on Emily, in a hospital corridor wearing a floral robe with a balloon tied around my wrist.

Emily, who is totally organized, is tsk-tsking over my paintings, drafts, newspapers, art magazines, piles of papers on the floor. Harry, sitting on a chair, comments that his office is also a mess and that he's a "slob too." Emily opens the ancient refrigerator and dumps old food into a huge garbage bag. "No wonder you're sick all the time," she says. "All this moldy food and rotten cheese!"

"It's not rotten," I feebly call out. "I melt it for sandwiches."

"Filthy," she murmurs, lecturing about the virtues of cleanliness, and how "no man will put up with a slob."

"And where is Mr. Wonderful?" Harry asks.

"In New York on a business trip."

Emily wrinkles her nose. "That man will disappear at the first sight of trouble. All he cares about is his dog."

"He's a loving father and grandfather."

"So what does that do for you? Is he loving to you?"

She continues to lecture that I need to "buck up" and

meet better men, that my career isn't everything, and that I need to "settle down." "Marv is a no-show—a silly, no-good juvenile."

"Amen," Harry says.

"He doesn't want a relationship, Mom. He only wants sex a few times a week. Meanwhile, he loves his frigid ex-wife. But you keep putting out!"

Harry nods in agreement.

I bite my tongue, thinking that she's been living with Harry six years and so far no proposal. While she's lecturing me to "take hold of my life," I remember Emily at twelve, standing on a box in the kitchen, rinsing dishes, baking banana bread in coffee cans, cleaning, and ironing. Always the responsible one. She dropped out of college and took a job as a maid, baking scones in the evening and selling them at local cafés, building her business. Years later, she went back to school, studied creative writing, as I had, and graduated from San Francisco State University with honors. She writes short stories about her mother and tries to sell them.

"Tomorrow, Mom, I'll bring a bag of my scones and some nice jam. Now go to sleep and don't get up. You're no spring chicken. All you need to do is fall. I'll leave the night-light on." She watches me a minute, as if making sure I'm all right. Then she gives me a big, wet kiss. I inhale the fresh smell of her ivory skin.

"I love you," I murmur, my tongue so thick I can't say the words.

"We love you too, Anny," Harry says. "We'll bring Fred to see you."

The door closes.

I now slide into a medicated, silent, dark sleep. I dream that I try to fly, but my wings turn to paper and I float down.

Chapter 20

Mr. X is not, as usual, standing by the car, ready to open the door for me. So I know tonight he'll be distant. When he is eager to see me, on his best behavior, he stands by the passenger door to help me into the car. When he's preoccupied with someone else, he doesn't drink vodka. In the movie, he doesn't hold my hand, and afterward, he drives me right home. He doesn't kiss me, but he gives his same dismissive "good luck with everything" speech.

Mr. X disappears on the weekends. I notice a pile of airline tickets on his coffee table, itineraries for various trips—

I post a blog called "Who Is the Real Mr. X?" I get thousands of responses.

Dear Anny: I have a Mr. X. He's vain, and tells me he loves me, then doesn't call. Can you help me?

Dear Anny: I'm a renaissance woman, I climb mountains and have credentials in law, and my newest adventure is to fly a hang glider. I want love, but the boomer-plus men I meet can't even walk up the stairs, let alone a mountain, yet they want a thirty-year-old. Do you think the Viagra generation treats age like a disease?

Dear Anny: I like your Mr. X column. I am a very active seventy-one-year-old veterinarian and love sex and would like to get your thoughts on how to discuss with my older lovers why they are not successful in promoting my climax.

A week later the neck crisis is over, but I'm wearing the brace. I've gone weeks without hearing from Marv, since before he left for a business trip to Mexico, then he calls out of the blue. I tell him about my neck and he sounds concerned. He asks if he can come over.

"Well, for a while," I say, surprised after what happened last time. "But I'm still wearing a neck brace, and I can't really visit long."

"Nine o'clock," he says, explaining that he's having dinner with a business partner first.

I try to put makeup on my face, a little shadow on my eyelids, but I can't bend to put something nice on. I'm wearing my black sweats and huge, loose sweatshirt.

At precisely nine, he arrives with a large package, the scent of his cologne drifting behind him. He looks elegant as usual, wearing a camel cashmere coat and a white cash-mere turtleneck. I'm glad to see him, but he seems ill at ease, anxious, complaining that he had trouble parking, couldn't find a parking place. He sighs. "I'm sorry you're going through this." He kisses me on the lips. "Arthritis, you said?"

I nod. "But it will go away soon."

He frowns, then says, "I brought you a gift."

"How nice." I tear open the red paper, excited that he actually brought me a gift. It's a blue crystal vase.

"I love it," I say, moved by this gesture.

"I found it in a curio shop. It wasn't cheap. But I thought you'd like it."

"Yes, thank you." I love the way his eyes get squinty when he's smiling. "It will look great on my glass table. I want to fix up my place."

He smiles. "Lovely roses," he says, glancing at the lavender flowers next to my sofa bed.

"So how was the gem show?" I ask after a long silence.

He looks confused.

"Your business trip to Mexico."

"Oh, that," he says with a shrug. "It was tiring. I lost a bid on an exquisite raspberry argyle diamond. It was perfect," he says, sighing wistfully.

"I'm sorry," I murmur.

He sits very straight, like a soldier before battle. His eyes are closed, closing me out. I tell him how lonely I've been and afraid. "The emergency room was awful. Suddenly I felt terrified about getting older and maybe ill."

"Nothing wonderful about age," he says, looking irritated.

"I think age is a gift."

"I think old age is a curse."

Silence

"Anny, why don't we go to Bolinas next weekend. You can see my place and have a vacation. It'll be fun."

"I'd love to." My promises to act cold, to let him know I'm upset, vanish. I follow him into the hallway.

We kiss. We kiss passionately. At first I don't see Ryan standing at the top of the stairs. When I look up, Ryan looks embarrassed.

"Sorry," Ryan says. "I had a book I wanted to give you."

Before I can introduce Ryan to Marv, Ryan rushes down the stairs.

"I'll pick you up Friday at noon," Marv says loudly. "Bring a bathing suit."

Chapter 21

Wouldn't you know? Friday is so hot the shadows don't move. I hate the heat. Marv arrives with the top down on his convertible, looking cool and chic, wearing spick-and-span khaki shorts and a slick, white polo shirt. While my linen skirt is all wrinkled and the heat is frizzing up my hair.

He looks sheepish. "I hope you don't mind I brought Honey? She was in a kennel all last week."

"Sure, no problem," I say, getting into the car.

He drives to the freeway. Just sitting next to him, I get that breathless feeling. The drive is nice. But the sun is beating on my head and I'm getting a headache. My tongue is parched and my pale arms are turning red and mottled with prickly heat, unlike Marv's smooth, olive-tanned skin.

Honey sits between us, hogging most of the space, with a little red tag reading "Bolinas" dangling from her thin neck, and her little water bottle on the seat. I'm pushed to the side, and I wonder why Honey was in a kennel and Debra didn't take care of her. Marv rests his hand on my knee while he drives, and between talking to Honey, he raves about the scenery, comparing it to the French countryside. "But Paris is the most gorgeous," he says, turning to look at the grassy fields. "It's a city of love. Debra and I went there on our honeymoon. A place you go with someone you love, a city that appreciates beauty."

"Yes. I want to go with you," I say, ignoring that he once again talked about Debra.

"We will!" he bellows, his voice rising above the sound of the cars.

"I'd love to paint in Paris."

"Look at the greenery, Anny. Isn't it glorious?"

"I like the cows." I shout to the cows grazing in the fields, "Moo!"

"You're crazy."

"I won't eat beef. Those poor cows are taken to slaughter to feed rich, fat Republicans! Poor cows!"

He turns on his Frank Sinatra CD, singing along to "My Way." The scenery is beautiful and green, and flowers and roses grow along the fences. The air smells so fresh and I feel content and happy and optimistic about spending a long weekend together.

Finally, he drives up a narrow, treacherous road and I close my eyes; I can't look down, especially when he talks to Honey, who is now sprawled along his lap. Then he drives up a hill to a wooded area and stops his car in front of a tall, contemporary, redwood-and-glass house set between mountains and tall oak trees.

"Here we are," he says to no one.

"Wow," I say, admiring the beauty of the site.

He turns off the motor. Except for the gravel settling and the rustling of animals in the bushes, it's dead quiet. Carrying Honey, he walks ahead and leads me inside. I stop in the entry, gasping at the beauty. The thirty-foot ceilings are dramatic, and the several glass skylights slide open and let in the trees, sky, and sunshine. It's gorgeous, really something. Plump, beige chairs and sofas—and again, orchids everywhere. "God, it's magical," I say, placing my bag on a chair.

"Pretty good for a boy from Toledo," he says, looking pleased. "Come on, Anny, I'll show you around."

Holding my hand, he leads me through each room excitedly, pointing out the room he furnished for his granddaughter, with bunk beds and toys neatly arranged on shelves, then finally into a spacious, white master bedroom and dressing room and white, glass-walled bathroom, complete with wide skylights and his and her sunken white marble bathtubs and matching johns.

"A wonderful retreat," I murmur.

Impatiently he glances at his watch. "I booked massages in an hour."

"I've never had a massage. I'm not sure I want one."

"You'll love it, Anny. Also, bring your swimsuit. Afterward, we'll take a swim."

After I unpack my things, placing them neatly on the shelf in the marble bathroom, I rinse my face with cold water, freshen up, put my swimsuit in my tote bag, then meet Marv outside.

We start our hike up this steep, narrow hill surrounded by deep drops and wildflowers, to the spa on top of the mountain. It's so hot that I can't breathe, and I'm huffing and puffing, feeling slightly light-headed. Of course, Marv, pilly and self-absorbed, holding Honey, walks fast ahead of me. But I assure myself that later we'll have a great time, then talk. So meanwhile, I'm trying to act cool, as if it were not hot at all, and that my new sandals don't hurt and that my blister on my toe isn't getting worse.

Finally, we get to the top of the mountain, to the Spa of Peace. In the center of this humid courtyard, people with trancelike expressions on their faces lounge around thin waterfalls trickling into dusty ponds with a few sickly looking orange goldfish swimming around. The air smells like incense and facial cream.

"Hello, I'm Waters," says a nymph-type girl—about eighteen, with pale blond, silky hair that hangs like threads past her waist. She wears a white, see-through, gauzy toga, accentuating her slim, firm body. She gives us each a white terry robe and a key to the showers, where we are to take off all our clothes and put on the robes.

"I'm sorry," she says. "Dogs are not allowed at this spa."

He smiles charmingly. "Honey isn't like a dog."

"Sir," she protests. "I—"

"Listen, I'll give you fifty dollars to babysit Honey while we have our massages and a swim."

Reluctantly, she takes Honey from his arms, instructing us to go to the Serenity Room after we change to meet our masseurs.

This Serenity Room is so hot that I can't breathe, and steam frizzes my hair like a hat. Quickly, I undress, stuff my clothes into the locker, wrap myself in this huge, ugly white robe that hangs to my ankles, and slap on a pair of too large, pink rubber thongs.

A Tibetan chant echoes solemnly from overhead speakers, really depressing, and all these men and women who look like cadavers in their white robes sit around awaiting their massages.

Marv makes his entrance, and of course he looks great in his white robe—his bare legs tanned, his hair shining silver. But he's in a mood; he's polite, but not here. He looks through me, as if I were an apparition. While I sit crouched up on the chair, covering my too white legs, which are speckled with age spots, making small talk about the "delicious scent of the nearby orange blossoms," his eyes are closed, as if he's closing me out.

"I'm Helmut, Ms. Applebaum's masseur," says a giant-size man with a wide face, tiny eyes, and a thick neck. He speaks in a thick German accent. He wears white, gauzy pajamas and blue paper slippers, and he's built like a moose.

"I'm Tai, Mr. Rothstein's masseur," says a waiflike Chinese boy wearing strands of turquoise and Mohawk-styled hair.

Marv barely kisses me on my lips, dutifully, like a bored husband. We agree to meet at the pool after the massage. I watch him strut, his shoulders back, head high, as he walks with Tai to his designated room.

This massage thing is a nightmare. I'm lying facedown, naked on a narrow table with a thin sheet over me. My face is jammed into this hole, the blood rushing to my head. Helmut is pounding my back and my neck, and I feel as if the top of my head were swelling up.

"I have arthritis in my head," I say. "Please, don't touch my neck."

"No such ting as arthritis in za head."

"I feel dizzy," I say, my voice muffled.

"You feel deezy because your circulation is bad," he says, continuing to pound my neck.

I try to take my mind off the torture I'm going through. I can't help but wonder why Marv seems so . . . distracted? Not that he's rude or anything; he's a master at polite silence, charming without saying anything. Trouble is, neither of us is being honest, is really talking to the other.

I close my eyes, remembering a month ago, when we went

to dinner and a movie. He was ice-cold and never touched me, not even holding my hand. I didn't say anything, figuring his new diamond deal didn't go through. Then, after the movie, instead of going to his house as we always do, he dropped me off at my place, explaining that he had an early doctor's appointment. "Thanks for a beautiful evening," he had said, as if I were a stranger. So as usual, instead of saying, *Hey! Mister! What's the problem?*, I went upstairs and wrote "Thanks for a Beautiful Night," about Mr. X's inability for intimacy, that he was probably cheating, but that he still wanted me too. But then I remembered that recently he confided that his PSA count was up, and I wondered if he was ill. Impossible to tell, though, since he's at the doctor's every minute, and even a slight cold can put him in a mood.

"So ve finish," says Helmut. When he leaves the room, I get up and put on the robe and sandals, feeling dizzy and sore. Tripping along the narrow path, I hurry to the showers and change into my one-piece, black Calvin Klein bathing suit. In front of this three-way mirror, I study my body, disgusted with the cellulite on my thighs. Not to mention the widening part on my head where my hair is thinning, and from the side, in the mirror—maybe it's the light—I notice a tiny bald spot, like the one my grandmother had.

Although Marv knows every inch of my body, I can't help but think that standing in the sunlight in a bathing suit is different from being naked in candlelight and moonlight. Okay, so what? Buck up. It's about time he sees me as I am.

• • •

jump into the pool as fast as I can, the cool water sooth-ing my sunburned arms. I float on my back, watching a blimp suspended in the sky and the clouds slowly form-ing shapes. Two athletic-looking, huge women in Speedo bathing suits and rubber caps sit by the pool, talking in Russian.

"Hello, Anny," Marv says, standing at the edge of the pool. Slowly, he removes his robe, dropping it on a chair, revealing his smooth, beautiful warrior body. He wears chic orange print trunks, tied by a drawstring at his slim waist. His skin is smooth as satin and golden, with not an ounce of extra fat on him. Silver hairs puff along his long, muscular chest.

Standing on the diving board now, aware that the Rus-sian women are staring at him, he pauses, his appraising eyes surveying the water, as if deciding where exactly he wants to dive. He holds his slim but muscular arms out, as if hugging his spot. In one swoop, he lifts to his toes, then dives into the pool, hardly making a splash, and gracefully swims two laps, his head moving side to side.

Wanting to show off my swimming abilities, I swim along with him, but my neck hurts and the chlorine burns my eyes. Treading water in the middle of the pool, we hold each other, spinning around. I'm shouting, "Hey. You're superman!" like a simp, flirting like crazy. But something is missing—a disconnect, I think, assuring myself that we just need to spend more time away, to share more things. This is our first.

"Did you swim a lot in Mexico?" I ask, trying not to gulp water.

"Some," he says, splashing water on his face.

"They say the water in Mexico is warm and beautiful."

He shrugs, then swims one more lap. I'm treading water, my legs moving as if I were riding a bicycle, assuring myself that it's all in my head, that I'm only imagining he's lying. He swims a few more laps, then he gets out of the pool, his hands smoothing his silver hair into place. Quickly I get out of the pool and slip on the robe.

"Let's get Honey and take the tram back. It's too hot to walk," Marv says. "I'm cooking tonight."

"Wow, nice."

We hurry to the offices where Waters is holding Honey. As soon as the dog sees Marv, she is trembling and howling and licking his face.

"I'm afraid Honey was not a good girl," Waters says in a thin voice. "She bit my arm. See this red spot?"

"Oh, she just gave you a love tap," he says, barely glancing at the poor girl's red arm. "She's always a good girl. Aren't you, Honey?"

Still consoling the yappy dog, Marv leads me to this tiny tram thing and we get in. Slowly, rocking back and forth, it descends along the edge of the mountain. I'm sitting in the back, squished in, and Marv and Honey sit up front. Marv comforts the scared dog, whispering what "a good girl" she's been. Overheated, my neck killing me, I hold on to the sides, fearful I'm going to fall.

Back at the house, Marv quickly changes into these neat gray sweats and T-shirt from Paris, looking all tan and gorgeous. "You take your time, Anny. I'm taking Honey and we're going to the store. Anything you want?"

"No, just you," I say like a sap. "I'll miss you."

"Miss you back," he says, shutting the door.

When I hear his car back from the driveway, I run the bathwater in the white marble tub, pouring in an incredible mango bubble bath. When the bubbles are almost to the top, I soak in the bath, my body submerged, thinking that tonight will be different, and that, after all, this is our first travel trip together. As I soak in the tub, I watch the sun slowly fade into twilight, until shadows fall along the lawn outside. Then I get out of the tub and dress for the evening.

I hear Honey's yowl and Marv's footsteps. Trying to move swiftly, careful not to leave my things all over the counters the way I do at home, I dress in snug, white jeans and a white, off-the-shoulder top that Emily loaned me. I arrange my hair into a low ponytail and stick a rhinestone butterfly in the side. A touch of makeup. My feet are swollen from the heat, so I decide to go barefoot. Last, I clasp a silver chain of butterflies around my ankle. I'm ready for the night. I go into the kitchen, where Marv is making drinks and arranging caviar and salmon on a platter. The stereo is on and Tony Bennett sings "I Left My Heart in San Francisco."

"You look pretty," he says, putting our drinks on the table. Next to the caviar and salmon, Brie and crackers are arranged on a wide ceramic plate next to a small bowl of olives and celery sticks. The glass roof is slid back, and the sky is so beautiful—stars poking the darkening sky like pins and fireflies darting like tiny lights.

"It's peaceful here," I say, sitting next to him. I sip my drink, light-headed now.

"I'm happy you're here," he says after a long silence.

"Me too."

He drinks his drink and pours more vodka in my glass.

"Did you see Frida Kahlo's house in Mexico?" I ask after a long silence.

"No. I was busy doing business."

"Diamonds."

"Kiss me." He pulls me closer. We kiss passionately, and I'm feeling no pain, even my headache is numb. By now the room is dark, except for the glow from the moon shaping in the sky, and I feel intoxicated from the drink, the sun, the moon, in the tranquillity of twilight and him.

"Don't get drunk," he says, taking the glass from me. "You had a lot of sun today."

.   .   .

After a lovely dinner—salmon, endive salad, prawns, and berry pie—we undress and get into bed. The air is still hot and the air-conditioning isn't working. Marv wants to watch a movie—he loves German war films—so in bed, all snuggled up, we watch this tedious, subtitled German film. Like a young boy engrossed in playing soldiers, he's totally absorbed. But my sunburn hurts, and the room is hot, and I can hardly breathe. Plus insects are biting my skin and I'm swelling up. Not to mention Honey is in bed with us—again.

The movie ends. It's 2:00 a.m. Marv clicks off the television, and except for the sound of crickets and insects tapping the windows, it's quiet.

"Let's go in the hot tub," he says after a long moment.

Stark naked, we make our way in the dark. God forbid he should turn on a light. "We need to preserve the lights," he repeats, while I'm groping along the edge of the wall, nearly blind without my contact lenses. God, it's awful. I feel as if I were a kid blindfolded, playing Pin the Tail on the Donkey, my hands grasping the air as I try to maintain my balance.

"My God—you can't see?" Marv nervously shouts. "Anny, why can't you see?"

"I don't have my contacts on, and I feel like I'm falling in space."

"I've got you, Anny," he says in a soothing voice. "Just

hold on. That's right. One more step. Two more steps. That's right. I've got you."

Finally, we're plopped in the hot tub. *Hot* isn't the word. It's so hot I can't breathe and feel I'm going to faint, and the water is bubbling and gurgling. "The water is too hot," I say, holding on to Marv. "It makes me dizzy."

"You make me dizzy," he says, holding me tight.

We kiss, and his mouth tastes like chlorine, and in the moonlight his face is silver. Then we're kissing passionately, my breasts flopping in the water like waves, my legs clasped around his waist. He tries to penetrate me, but he's soft. "Not to worry. It's the water. It doesn't matter," I say.

"Make it hard," he says anxiously.

He keeps pushing my hand along his penis, telling me to suck it, squeeze it, and the gurgling water is giving me a migraine. So finally I say I'm exhausted. "Too much sun."

"C'mon," he sighs. "Let's go to bed."

Back in bed, Marv turns off the light, takes a moment to settle himself with the pillows, leaving me with the hard, rubbery pillow.

"That's never happened before," Marv sighs.

"Did you take your Viagra?"

"What?" he snaps. "What are you talking about? I don't need Viagra."

"I'm sorry—"

"Let's go to sleep," he snaps. "End of conversation."

Soon, he's snoring. But Honey is growling at me and my sunburn hurts and I'm lying awake. All night I lie awake, my eyes on the fading moon, wondering how it is that every time I start to feel close to this man, he slips away from me.

When I wake, Marv's side of the bed is empty. I look at the clock, horrified. It's almost 10:00 a.m. I hear Marv's voice from the kitchen.

I take a shower. I wash and rinse my hair, letting the water drape over my face. The day is stifling hot, one of those days when it's so hot that the clouds stay in one place, like giant puffs of white air.

I dress quickly, noting that Marv's side of the bathroom is spotless, not one item out of place, while my toiletries, combs, and jars of antiaging cream are all over the counter. I slip on a long-sleeved, white T-shirt, long khaki shorts, and flat sandals. I tie my still-damp hair into a ponytail—no makeup.

Marv is in the kitchen, slicing oranges. He looks agitated.

"Good morning," I say, pouring coffee into a cup.

"Guess what, Anny," he says, slicing more oranges. "Waters called. She claims that she had to go to the hospital and get a tetanus shot, and now she wants me to pay for it."

"You should pay. She doesn't have anything. I saw the red mark on her arm."

"Honey doesn't bite!" he snaps, arranging the oranges onto

a plate. "That girl must have done something terrible to poor Honey. She knows who I am, and she just wants money."

"Honey has nipped my hands many times, Marv. She's a brat."

"You have to know how to touch her. You don't know how to touch her."

I struggle not to tell him that he's cheap and that his moods are hot and cold and I want to leave.

At the glass table, set with a bowl of wildflowers and linen napkins, we eat breakfast. I pick at my fruit bowl, irritated by his selfishness and temperamental moodiness. Acting as if I'm not here, he's eating his cheese omelet, sighing and remarking how much better his cooking is than that of the "fucking overpriced restaurants."

"It's hot today," I say. "I hate the sun."

"So you've said." He concentrates on eating his eggs. He eats neatly, pushing half of the omelet to the side of the plate.

"I want to go to this winery today, in Napa," he says after a tense silence. "There's a fine French wine I want to buy. I tasted it last week in Paris—" He stops talking.

Silence. A heavy silence.

"You weren't in Mexico," I say. "You were with Debra in Paris."

"It was a sudden business trip," he says with a sigh. "Debra is very good at selling diamonds. In the past, she often accompanied me on big sales."

"You lied!" I say, glad for the sudden shock on his face. "You took your other woman to Paris! All this time—you have a girlfriend? So talk!"

He sighs. "Anny, I took Debra to help me make the final deal on the yellow diamond. It's not what you think. She's family."

"And what am I? Your Monday-night fuck? Your ho? Your booty call?"

"I don't have sex with anyone but you."

"Of course you do. Marv, I hate liars. I hate that you keep me compartmentalized. I hate that you don't take me to Paris. I hate that you keep me separate. I hate that when you're with me you only give me some of you—"

"I care for you, Anny. What we have is special, but I'm not in love with you."

"Isn't love on any level about honesty and intimacy? Don't you dare insult me! As if 'not in love' means you have the right to decieve me? How dare you! You don't even know who I am! You don't know that my column is based on you, everything about you. You're Mr. X. So did you think I was so in love with you? All along I used you for material. You would have known if you had read it. I've been on the radio, speaking gigs. All about you."

He blinks several times as though taking in what I said. Then he glances at his watch and looks back at me, as if deciding something.

"I've read your silly column," he says, a cruel expression on his face. "I'm not going to see you anymore, Anny."

"Good. Because I have no intention of answering your calls again. Please take me home."

On the way home, Marv's hands clutch the steering wheel tightly. The silence between us is palpable. He drives fast. As if I'm not here, he talks on his cell phone, to his son, making plans to meet for dinner, acting as if nothing were wrong. Except that when he's nervous, he acts the opposite. I keep my head turned as if looking out the window at the cows, thinking back on every word he said. Suddenly I remember the first night I was at his home, when he poured cognac, he'd wistfully said, a yearning look in his eyes, that *Paris is for lovers*. These words shock me. Shock me into reality. Then I remember the blue vase that he gave me. He had said he bought it in Mexico, but the sticker on the bottom said it was made in France. At the time I hadn't thought anything of it.

By the time Marv stops the car in front of my apartment, it's late afternoon, and lazy shadows invade the sunlight. A cool breeze blows the roses out front. I wish Ryan were home from his trip so that I could tell him what happened and how miserable I feel.

I get out of the car and rush into the apartment, not looking back to wave one more time.

Chapter 22

Monday morning I'm at an emergency meeting with Dr. Indira. Today, at my request, I sit on a chair facing her. She sits straight. She wears a pink sari over a black turtleneck sweater and pants. Her thick silver hair is braided. A huge gold bracelet is on her dainty wrist. I've been telling her every detail about what happened in Bolinas.

"Thank God it's over," I say.

"Is it?"

"Of course! I never want to see him again. I should never have gone away with him. He's a liar and he's indifferent to everything about me except for my vagina. He pretended he was in Mexico on a buying trip, but this time he slipped up. He was with his ex-wife in Paris."

I open my purse and take out my paper bag. I blow into it, my cheeks puffing out. I wait until I stop crying.

"When we had sex, I could have had a bag over my face, and it didn't matter that I was there. He's not in love with me, he says, like I don't exist. The prick uses Viagra like it's a sport. A form of entertainment, he—"

"Why did you stop?"

I am sobbing, pulling the rest of the Kleenex from the box. "I knew from the beginning he was committed to the ex-wife. I felt it in my bones. God, I knew he wasn't emotionally available, yet I persisted in imagining that he'd fall madly in love with me, run off to Paris with me, and we'd live happily ever after."

"Is that what you really wanted?"

"In my fantasy."

"You had that in your marriage. You had the beautiful suburban home, an affluent husband who adored you, a community, a lovely daughter, yet you have told me that you were unhappy."

"I never said I was unhappy with the marriage. Just with myself."

"It's the same thing," she quietly says. "You need to define what it is exactly that you want. Maybe you love Marv because he could only give you a tiny bit of himself? Maybe you don't want more? But he gave you Mr. X. You're becoming a recognized columnist, and financially independent."

"But I wanted romantic love. He aroused in me sexual feelings that I never felt with Donald, or for anyone, but I wanted the emotional connection too. Who does he think he is?"

I wait, picking at a loose string on my blouse. The room is stuffy. "Marv loves sex with me, loves my orgasms, and I expected him to be as caring outside the bedroom. But he's a horny teenage boy who masturbates on me. I've had it." I take a deep breath. "I have to resolve Marv."

"It's not Marv you have to resolve. It's yourself. When you do that, you'll know if you want to be with Marv."

I blow into my paper bag.

"We have to stop," she says.

I hurry to the door, tripping on the loose shoelace from my high-top basketball shoes, and turn the lock three times to the right, then to the left, then rush down the stairs, to the daylight.

I walk fast up the hill, huffing and puffing, and thinking about the therapy session. Dr. Indira is right. Just as I hoarded things for my boxes, to keep Marv, even thinking I could mold him to my needs, I chose not to face my truths or to believe Marv when he said he didn't love me. So is it true that all I want is Mr. X? Or was that my only alternative? Either way, this time there is no going back.

As I pass Sacramento Street, the chic outdoor cafés, and arty jewelry shops, I recall Donald and I sitting at Rose's Café, drinking espressos, and shortly after that day I found the Viagra in his pants pocket. And suddenly for the first time I feel relieved that Marv and I are over, but also sad.

It's over.

Totally over.

The following days are hard. I'm in pain. No matter how imperfect my relationship with Marv was, I felt a deep connection and it's gone. I'm unable to sleep, awake at dawn, going over every detail of our every time together. Until I feel less vulnerable, figure out my feelings for Marv, I can't write about him. "It's over," I tell Monica. She urges me to take my time, to continue to write about romance in the boomer set. So I bury myself in work, pursue new profiles, set up new interviews, and write more columns. I interview sixty-plus women about the older men they date. I continue to research the singles sites and print out the profiles of the sixty-plus men, all claiming to be fabulous and brilliant. I interview a screenwriter who wants a travel companion, a potter who wants me to go to the mountains with him and write poetry, widowers on the make, affluent men with new hairpieces, their foreheads smooth from Botox, their skin orange from tanning salons, who think cosmetic surgery is a way of reinventing themselves. Still, they talk about finding the perfect relationship. The "Big R," they say, wistfully sighing.

I think everything is going fine, but then one month after the trip to Bolinas, on my daily walk to Starbucks, I see Marv driving his convertible with the top down. It stops in front of the Polk Street Florist. Breathless, I stand behind a doorway, butterflies in my stomach, watching as he hurries inside, then leaves, carrying a bouquet of yellow tulips. As I watch him drive away, his car radio up high, I feel angry. Angry and inspired.

I rush home to the computer, and easily I write "Breakup!"— about Bolinas and my hurtful breakup with Mr. X.

At times, I see his face in the clouds, his body in the shadows. I watch the cars for a sign of Mr. X—I stand in a doorway, watching Mr. X exit a florist's shop on California Street. He's carrying a bouquet of yellow roses. Who are they for? I've never seen yellow roses at his home. My heart is beating fast—

My column "Breakup" causes fan frenzy. Once again I'm receiving e-mails from around the country. The fans tell me about their breakups with their partners and want to know if I'm going to ever see Mr. X again. Some fans post blogs, taking bets on whether Mr. X goes back to me or to his ex-wife. The column is going so great that I'm not obsessing about the breakup with Marv. Then the kicker: as I sip my morning coffee on a sunlit Monday morning, I open a copy of the *Gazette*, the socialite paper. And there he is. Under the heading "Opera Gala of the Year," there's a full-page, blown-up picture of Marv and an attractive, tall, much younger woman. She has long, dark hair and a narrow, haughty face. Even in the photograph I can see she's wearing a huge diamond necklace and earrings. They don't say her name; only that Marv donated a diamond to the opera gala.

I close the paper. I feel stunned. I had fantasized that he was pining away for me too. Now I know it isn't true. I was so in lust that I wouldn't look at the truths. All I knew was that I wanted him. And clearly I see that I tried to make what we had into something not possible. I've always done this. With Donald, to avoid rejection, I looked the other way. I let Emily take over, be the parent. I need to clarify my truths first, know who I am, what I want, so this won't happen again.

As the weeks pass, I continue to explore not only boomer dating, but also the ups and downs of aging; I study how the media reward glitz, face-lifts, how they ignore the elderly and seniors. I hate the way television profiles seniors dancing around the kitchen, clutching bottles of Caltrate. I write more about ageism, and Monica runs my articles separately from the column. I maintain that aging is not a dead end, but a series of beginnings, reaching for something new.

I'm invited to speak about boomer dating at different venues, and to be on local television shows. I write a series of talks about my perceptions of aging. The *Star Reporter* offers me more money if I write a column for them. I say no. I remember how rude they were when I had pitched them years ago, and how Monica gave me a chance.

I decide to work harder on my boxes and paintings.

This evening, I'm working on a large canvas. First, with a stick of charcoal, I draw an elongated figure of a woman. Next, I dip a brush into pure white paint, painting her body white, accentuating shadows with gray. In pale gray I paint a filmy, see-through dress, slit on one side, her long legs and thighs provocatively visible, the dress flirtatiously drooping from her bare shoulders. I work fast now, painting her stilt-like high heels black. She is wild, and about to step from the canvas and devour life. A filmy black veil falls over her white face, her eyes smudged with secrets. I'll call it *Natasha Is Out.*

The music is up high. Billie Holiday blows my mind—her emotions pour through each note.

I paint until the footsteps upstairs are quiet, until the room turns so cold I shiver, until paint smears my glasses and I can't see.

I drop the brushes into the bin of water. I observe the painting, figuring out what it needs. Who is the woman in the painting? Why does she look so sad? Unresolved?

I place a plastic tarp over the canvas. I will continue to paint her, to see what evolves.

Before I go to bed, I sit by the window, looking at the lovely drawing that Ryan sent me. It is in black ink, on a small white card. It is of a mountain. "May we climb the next one together," he writes.

The air is still tonight. The night crawls along the houses across the street, like cats. Destiny is a band leading your dreams. I imagine that the soul is clear and squishy and has its separate existence. It never dies.

Chapter 23

The following week Monica calls and asks to see me at her office. "News to tell you," she says.

I'm wearing my new ankle-length, black sweater coat, and high heels. When I arrive, Monica kisses me on the cheek and she tells me that "Prozac or Passion" outdid all other sales. "Anyhoo," she says, exhaling smoke, "the column is going to be syndicated nationally."

"Wow! Are you serious?"

She nods. "Sure am. More money for you, and for me."

"I'm excited."

"The fans miss Mr. X. They love the boomer dating columns, but they write that they want to know what happened with Mr. X. I want you to resume writing about Mr. X. I think the issue of the disconnect between sex and emotional communication is important. The blog is filled with that issue."

"I'm not seeing him. It's really over."

"So make it up. You can do it. But we need to wrap up the Mr. X series. Then you can write what you want. Meanwhile, do some research. You know him."

"I'll think of something."

"Until then, just continue writing about love after sixty." She brushes cigarette ash from her black Kate Spade sweater. "Kate Nielson from talk radio called me. She wants you on her call-in show on Friday. Good advertisement for the paper."

"Sure."

"You've put this paper on the map: syndication, awards, the whole schmear. Show me what you've got."

That night I meet Lisa and Janet for drinks at Myrtles Bar on Polk Street, a neighborhood bar with sawdust on the floor and rowdy blue-collar guys watching basketball on the overhead television. I tell them my good news and we click glasses.

"You're on your way, honey," Janet says.

"Has *he* called?" Lisa wants to know.

"It's only been a few weeks. And I don't care," I say, feeling defensive.

"Honey, be cool," Janet advises. "Don't call him. Serves him right."

"Of course I'm not calling him. It's over. And he knows

that my columns are about him. That I wasn't hanging around him because I trusted him on any level."

"Well, who knows?" Lisa says. She wears all turquoise blue. "He may have read your columns and even loved being Mr. X."

"Who knows is right," Janet snaps, drinking bourbon over ice. "Could also be that he didn't give a rat's ass about Anny's columns or anything but her vagina. Oy. These Viagra boomer guys are a nightmare. They want one thing. We're supposed to lick their balls, make tuna casseroles, clean the toilets. They don't know we moved on. We're a new ageless generation. They're stuck in the old one."

"Yuk. Enough with the balls," I say.

"Like chewing bubble gum," Janet says.

"I don't care if I ever see another penis again," Lisa says. "It's so ugly, like a scrunched-up smiley face. John can't do it, but it's fine with me. He loves me."

"All along all he wanted was sex," I say. "Yes, it was good sex. But I don't want good sex with indifference. It won't work. Plus, he didn't, doesn't acknowledge holidays, birthdays, my work. Like I don't exist."

"My vagina has shrunk into a tiny hole. So who needs sex?" Lisa says.

Janet rolls her eyes.

"Belgium, Mexico, France, whatever," I say. "He has a woman, and a much younger one. Yet he had the nerve to pursue me sexually."

"He wants you for the good sex," Lisa says.

"When he wants it," I say, feeling angry. "He doesn't care if I fuck a harem as long as he gets his fix."

"All the boomer guys say that, honey," Janet says. "Trick is to get a good one to marry you. Then you have health, life, and emotional insurance."

"So are we just like old dogs in heat?" I ask.

"Dogs don't have the problems we have. They do it, bark their heads off, and then move on to the next."

"Girls! Enough! I have an announcement," Janet says. A glow comes to her face. "I met this Hungarian. He moves furniture for Macy's. A hunk. A widower too, and my age. He's wonderful. You should see me flirt. Also, the man can do it without Viagra."

"You go, girl," I say, hugging her.

"I don't understand what he's saying half the time, but he brings me chewing gum. He knows I like Dentyne."

"I smell a rat," Lisa says.

"The rat you smell," Janet says, glaring at Lisa, "is the moron guy you're seeing. He gives 'How to Love' seminars at his penthouse, so he can meet all the young girls. Meanwhile he files bankruptcy and makes you pay for expensive dinners. In my book, if they lay, they pay."

Lisa shrugs. "He cuddles though. Anyway, I have an announcement too. Although it's less exciting. I'm having a hip replacement next month."

"Oh, we'll be with you," we say.

She blinks several times. "My son will be with me. Not to worry."

"You can depend on us," Janet says.

"Amen," I say.

"Let's lock it," Lisa says. We lock fingers.

The weather turns cooler, and fog blows into the city like lonely gasps. These darker, cooler days make me hibernate—go inward in a deeper way. When I'm not writing and painting, I go to the museums, study the paintings, read everything I can about the artists I admire. Ryan is still away, but he continues to send me postcards, e-mails, and sometimes he calls. He's a good friend and I miss his company.

At night, I rent films on Netflix, studying plot, dialogue, acting. I want to improve my speaking and acting skills, and I join a small acting group at the Marsh Theater. I love the kids, the dreams in their eyes, their indifference to convention. Acting is a way of getting close to the emotions.

I visit convalescent homes and interview men and women. I watch them folk dance, flirt, and fight over who sits with whom. Some show me photographs of deceased loved ones, the past shining on their faces like romance. Only their bodies are old, not their spirits. Age is like old trees; they keep growing and are simply versions of younger trees.

It's Thursday night, a windy, cold day. I'm at my computer finishing "Sage," a piece about how older people are treated as if they were invisible.

Dumbed down. No matter how old one is, the soul is young and the intelligence is keen. We must emphasize goals rather than antidepressants.

An hour later I finish the piece and close my computer. It's near 10:00 p.m. I feel restless and call Janet.

"Hello, honey, what's up?" she says.

I tell her about my piece on aging. We complain about the boomer men on the singles sites who want women no older than thirty. "One ugly man after the other," I tell Janet.

"Honey, that's what's out there."

"Even ugly men are jerks. Most of the boomer men are on the prowl, running around with their hairpieces, fake tans, and Viagra."

"Usually, you think the ugly men are the good guys," Janet muses. "They lie about their age. But the women cater to them, invite them out, blow them, make tuna casseroles. The men could have six heads, in diapers, and they're still in demand. Thank God I met Paul. He's a keeper."

"Amen. He sounds wonderful." I'm happy for Janet. "Anyway, these boomer-plus guys make Marv look like an Adonis."

Janet sighs. "Marv is bad news. You paid a big price for your Mr. X."

"Anyway, Ryan is home and he's invited me to meet him for lunch tomorrow."

"Go for it. He's a doll."

"He's a friend. I'd rather have a good friend than an unreliable lover."

"Honey, no such thing as friends with these men. Have fun."

Chapter 24

The next day I'm on my way to Ryan's studio in China-town to meet him for lunch. The day is cold, and a thick, gray fog floats over the city. I walk through the Broadway tunnel, to Bush Street, then to Grant Avenue.

I arrive at Chinatown and it's like another world. Tourists ride colorful double-decker buses along Bush Street's narrow hills, and cable cars struggle up steep hills, tourists hanging from the sides. The cobblestone streets are so narrow you have to walk single file. Shops, restaurants, and houses with pink and red, sloped, shingled roofs appear like stacked building blocks, one on top of the other. Ducks hang from strings in store windows, and fresh produce is displayed in stalls. Colorful silks, rubber spiders dangling from wires, fans, pearls, and jade are displayed in shop windows. I remember taking Emily to Chinatown as a child, buying her fans, and then at Mein's Restaurant above an old temple eating chow mein. Everything—people, houses, products—is jumbled in Chinatown, like some old world, and it's always full of excitement and activity.

At the end of Grant Avenue, I arrive at a gray, square industrial building, where fortune cookies are manufactured. It is set between two restaurants with red, sloped roofs. Ryan leased the building a few years ago. Rents are cheap in Chinatown, and Ryan speaks Mandarin and Chinese.

I ride a shaky freight elevator to the top floor, holding my breath. Ryan, wearing his usual black jeans and a black shirt, is waiting at the top. His face lights up as he smiles. He hugs me tight, murmuring that he's glad to see me.

"You look great, Anny. Come in. I have some photographs to show you." He walks ahead of me. His keys attached to his wide leather belt make a clinking sound.

He leads me into a large, light-filled room with tall industrial windows that face a Chinese temple and a row of crooked stairs and buildings. The odors of pork buns and steamed rice sift through the open windows.

"This is marvelous," I say, looking around.

He smiles. Gray speckles his hair. "I'll make some tea. Look around."

At a small, makeshift kitchen, Ryan makes tea. Tools, camera equipment, and Apple computers are arranged on a long wood table. Everything is neat.

I admire the photographs on the walls. Huge black-and-white blowups of Barcelona's fabulous range of Gaudí's architecture, next to gardens in France and Italy. His photographs are dramatic in the way that a Robert Mapplethorpe photograph is simple, pure, white, revealing the stark essence. Ryan has a huge array of interests—bees, forests, the sea, and politics. He's a member of left-wing political groups and photographs the political leaders.

"The Eskimo girl's eyes are haunting," I say. "You caught her essence, startling against the beauty of the landscape. Why does she look so sad?"

"She isn't sad. She's resigned. That's what I tried to capture."

We sit on deck chairs, drinking persimmon tea. Steam clouds our faces. For a while we don't talk. There is so much I want to ask him about, talk about, but I'm feeling content just being here in this wonderful room with him.

"So what's up, Anny? Update me."

"Well, the columns are going to be syndicated, but Monica wants more Mr. X columns and to wrap up the series."

"So what's the problem?"

"I'm not with Marv anymore. I need Marv in order to write the series."

"Anny, trust yourself. You can write without him."

"Manet always used a model. So did van Gogh."

"It's not their models that make their paintings great. It's their emotions. Create Mr. X from what you know about Marv, and you know a lot. You sold your soul to get Mr. X."

I sip the tea, thinking about what Ryan said.

"What happened with Marv?" he asks after a long moment.

"What didn't happen?" I tell him about Bolinas, about Marv's lie, about everything. Ryan listens intently, his hand lightly holding the cup of tea.

"You deserve better than that," he says. "Be with someone who wants to spend time with you."

"Some relationships, though not perfect, are an affair of the heart. Sometimes there are too many wounds—"

"That's hogwash, Anny," Ryan snaps. "You deserve it all. What you had with Marv was superficial."

I don't reply, knowing that this is true, knowing that I never wanted to face that Marv doesn't love me and that the only way I could be with him, like an addict wanting a fix, was to tell myself lies.

We finish drinking our tea. We talk about photography, its relationship to painting. "I think photography can capture what painting can't," I say. "And painting can capture details and ideas, but photography can capture what's not seen."

He looks reflective. "I have something for you. He jumps up and takes a lovely Lucite box from the table. Inside are dozens of tiny glass stars in different shapes. On top is an emerald-green glass ball.

"It's lovely," I say, delighted with this gift. "I love it. Thank you."

"You're all these stars. The green ball shows that sometimes life goes in another direction. Whenever you have a new wish, take a star out. It's your special box."

He touches the side of my face so gently, the way I've seen him touch a flower. "I made lunch reservations at the Dragon. The food is wonderful. Let's go. You'll feel better when you eat great food. It's great to see you, Anny."

The Dragon is crowded with tourists and Asian families getting ready to celebrate New Year's. It is dark inside. Huge murals of gold dragons shimmer on the walls. The carpets are deep red, and the waiters wear red satin jackets and black caps.

First, we eat sizzling-hot rice soup. Then Ryan orders various dishes—shrimp, fish, green vegetables, rice. The room is warm, and steam from the hot dishes covers the windows like mist. I'm enjoying sharing this meal with Ryan. He tells me about the show he's going to have in Ireland the following year. He maneuvers his chopsticks like a musician using a baton. He puts more prawns on my plate.

"Why Ireland?"

"It's a good assignment, but I'd also like to go back to my birthplace. I'm going to spend weeks walking and cycling among Ireland's highest mountains. I'm interested in the early Christian monasteries, Celtic forts, and medieval manors. I want to buy a castle and work there part-time—a great place for artists, and you can live cheap compared to here."

"Sounds like you have a plan," I say, tasting the prawns.

"I do. You're in it."

"You're crazy."

"This is nice, just talking." He smiles tentatively, like a boy caught somewhat off guard. He graciously pours hot jasmine tea into my cup. "So, tell me more about your ex-husband. What was he like?"

I pause, take a deep breath. "When I first met him, I thought he was Prince Charming. He was smart, hand-some . . . traditional. We were young." I feel wistful. "Anyway, that's the brief version."

He sighs. Then he kisses the palm of my hand. "Anny. You haven't been with the right man. I think I know you. Let's spend some time together while I'm here."

"Yes, let's."

"Don't go back to him, Anny."

We sit in a long silence.

Afterward, hand in hand, we walk along the streets, which are already gaining crowds for the parade that night. Gorgeous floats are in line along the narrow street, and the golden dragon is over two hundred feet long with yellow and red pom-poms along its six-foot head. Firecrackers are in the air and flashes of color explode in the darkening sky. Ryan snaps pictures of the Chinese families with their young children wearing colorful costumes, and of the Chinese boys preparing the pagoda float. He buys me a gold silk fan covered in tiny pink painted flowers. When I open it, there are strips of pearl inlay.

Ryan takes a photograph of me holding the fan, and we ask a tourist couple to take pictures of us. Then he has to go back to work as he's photographing the parade. We hug good-bye, and I walk home.

A few days later Ryan drops off the photographs he'd taken of me. He framed one of me holding the fan that he bought me, and I'm smiling flirtatiously. I look happy. It's as if Ryan caught what I was feeling and maybe didn't admit to myself. I wonder if we could be happy, if I care for him more than I want to. I place the photographs next to the Lucite box of glass stars and the little green ball.

It is evening and a light rain falls. I open the windows to let in the full moon. I play back my messages. I'm shocked to hear Marv's voice: "Please call back. I'm up late."

I'm shaking. I feel up, down, telling myself not to return the call. I clear my desk for the next day's work, then get ready for bed, assuring myself that I'm over him, and that I don't need to talk to him.

I sink into a dreamless sleep.

The next morning, near seven, the phone rings. This time, I pick it up.

"Anny," Marv nervously says. "I'm glad you picked up. Are you awake?"

I hold the phone tight.

"Please, Anny, I'd like to see you. Anny, please talk to me."

"I hear you," I groggily say.

"Please, Anny. Have dinner with me tonight. I need to talk to you."

"Marv, I'm really busy. It's over. We shouldn't— I—"

"Seven. I'll pick you up. It's important, Anny."

I get up, assuring myself that there's nothing wrong in just talking. After all, we did have a relationship. Plus, don't I need more material? But I know that I should walk away from this vain man who endlessly searches for youth and immortality. Who will never give me my storybook ending.

I conference-call Janet and Lisa. I confide that I'm meeting Marv. "He wants to talk," I explain.

"He's probably bored with the frigid superstar ex-wife," Lisa says.

"Talk? When a man says *talk*, it means 'fuck,'" Janet says. "If he weren't on Viagra and had a limp dick, he'd talk real. But as long as he can get his fuck fix, he has nothing to say."

"Same old thing. That's what he'll say. Don't waste your time," Lisa says.

"You girls are pessimistic."

"Be unavailable," they say.

It's evening. I finish dressing, turning one more time and looking at myself in the three-way mirror. I'm wearing a mauve cashmere sweater, with a midcalf black skirt, mauve stockings, and ankle boots with purple laces. I'm ready.

The phone rings. It's Marv. He's in the lobby. Usually he waits outside, either in the car or by the passenger door. He's as eager as I am, I tell myself.

Marv is looking all spiffy, wearing a gray turtleneck sweater and a long, black leather jacket. Smiling, he moves toward me, his arms out to hug me. Just then Ryan enters the lobby. He glances at us, then does a double take.

"Um, Marv, meet my neighbor Ryan," I say, pulling away from Marv's embrace.

"Oh, you're the guy who takes photographs," Marv says.

Ryan shrugs. "You're the guy who sells blood diamonds?"

"I don't sell blood diamonds. I sell diamonds," Marv corrects.

Ryan looks at me, confusion in his eyes, before hurrying down the hallway. I hear the door to his apartment slightly slam.

We're at the North Beach Restaurant, seated at Marv's usual table. The restaurant is festive, Miró prints cover the walls, and the sound of bartenders shaking cocktail shakers and dice thrown on the mahogany bar mingle with the cacophony of sounds from the open kitchen. We're sipping martinis. Since he picked me up, he's been especially attentive, hovering over my every word.

"I want you back, Anny."

I try to smile. I warn myself that he can be seductive and that it's over.

"Do you not want me back?" he says, looking tentative.

"I don't like the way you treated me. Like I'm not there. You run hot and cold. There have been too many hurts."

He sighs and looks sheepish, like a young boy caught stealing a cookie. "Anny, don't leave me. I need you."

"It would be more of the same, and then we'd both hate each other." I hesitate. "I wouldn't want you with Debra or any other woman. That's the way I am."

"I'm not with her anymore. I need you, Anny."

I finish my drink. "I'm not sure, Marv."

"Is it Ryan? He looks at you as if he owns you."

"Not at all. I just think it's impossible for us."

"I know. Of course." He kisses my hand. "I do love you, Anny. I do."

Our petrale sole comes. I can hardly eat. I know that this is the moment that I should walk away. I know this—know that he won't change, that to go back to him is going backward, but he's saying the words I've fantasized about, and my feelings are fluctuating from wanting to end it once and for all to imagining us as a real couple in love. But Marv has a way of making events and people exactly the way he wants, and then when the moment is gone, he disappears. I warn myself to be cautious.

"The fish is wonderful," I say, trying to keep us light.

"What about you, Anny? Do you love me?"

"What does love have to do with wanting a good and respectful relationship?"

"Give me another chance," he says. "Be with me, Anny. I can't live without you."

Wham. When he says those words, I melt. Everything changes. He's come around, I tell myself.

A half an hour later we're at Marv's house. I'm undressing as if there were a fire. Nothing matters, nothing matters except him, right here. Wow. Nothing else matters. I'm in another world. I can't help it. I jump into bed and we melt in each other's arms, and then there's nothing, nothing but us, but the feel of us.

"I've dreamed of this," he whispers, on top of me, kissing me passionately.

"Do it now," I whisper into his mouth.

"Ssshh . . . let's wait a bit, make it last. Let's make it last forever."

He tries to enter me, but, oh, dear God, he's soft, really soft—and here I am, my legs wound around his neck, and he's pushing and shoving and nothing, nada, nothing, and now he's not even kissing me, nothing—and slowly he pulls away, and my legs slowly go down, down like embarrassed children.

"I can't. God, I can't. Do it now."

We lie still for what seems forever. Marv is lying on his back. The moon is so close it almost touches the window, and gold light sprays Marv's taut face.

"It's the drinking," I say, kissing him. "We can spoon." I bury my face in his shoulder.

"I'm tired, I guess. I have a bad headache. Maybe from the vodka."

"Not to worry. Love is how you do the loving. It's not only about the sex." I hold him tighter.

"Anny, I left the night-light on if you get up during the night. There are cough drops in the drawer next to you. You cough a lot. Did you get the chest X-ray?"

"Soon."

"Anny, I know you like a soft pillow. Let me give you my soft pillow." He places it behind my head.

"I fly in my dreams," I say, snuggled in his arms.

"I float in a shallows, the current takes me," he says wistfully. "It's wonderful. I float forever, and I never age."

"Be careful." I kiss his mouth. "Like Icarus, if you go too near the sun, you'll disintegrate."

He kisses me on the mouth. "Good night, darling."

"Where is Honey?" I ask, my voice hollow.

"She's at the kennel. I have to go to Vegas for a gem show, then to New York on business. I'll be gone a couple of weeks."

"Why didn't Debra take Honey?"

"Debra is away."

He turns to his side and sleeps. He's shut off now. I can't sleep. I'm lying awake, staring at the lights floating on the ceiling, knowing I've once again been duped. He tosses, turns, sighs, and snores. Twice, murmuring his headache is worse, he gets up and goes into the bathroom. I hear the water running, hear him coughing, the sound of pills shaking in a bottle. He gets back into bed. His feet are cold.

The moon is gone now, and the sky is black. "I can't live without you," he said. So certainly he wouldn't lie at this point? Finally, I slip into a half sleep, letting my mind wander, riding a camel in the desert, swinging on a swing in Ireland, dancing a belly dance in Istanbul. Exotic lights and tall grasses cover my naked body, bracelets covered with stones clink along my arms, rings on my toes, silver chains on my ankles.

When his alarm goes off at 6:00 a.m. I quickly wake, and he jumps up. "We have to hurry and dress, Anny. I have an emergency business meeting this morning."

"Sure, uh-huh," I say.

He hurries into his bathroom. When I hear the shower, and Marv singing Frank Sinatra tunes, I look at the newspapers on the chairs. Not one *San Francisco Times.* There is no evidence that he's read my columns, or cares to. Nothing. Everything is neat, hidden as usual.

A towel around his waist, he comes into the room. "It's all yours, Anny."

"Thanks," I say, carrying my clothes, hurrying into the bathroom and locking the door. Steam lingers in the air and smells like his cologne. I turn on the shower, full force, pretending that I'm using it. Frantically, I search the medicine cabinet for the Viagra pills. Nothing. Quickly I dress in last night's clothes, wondering if he's really read my Mr. X columns, or that he doesn't believe a hoot that they have any significant audience.

I rinse my face with cold water and brush my hair with his brush, noticing the bottle of French perfume on the other side of the counter. Telling myself that I'm looking for trouble, I go into the kitchen. Marv is making espressos in his jumbo, red espresso machine. He's dressed in his dark, pinstripe, careful suit, white shirt, silver tie, his hair all slicked back. "Just the way you like it. Foam on top," he says formally, giving me a tiny glass cup of espresso. A thin slice of lemon rind floats on the top.

I sit on the tall stool, drinking the coffee, and watching as he makes eggs, lecturing that I need to eat better.

"So, have you read my Mr. X columns?"

"Mr. X is a cool guy," he says, spooning eggs onto his Versace, fancy plates. He sits next to me, his face close to the eggs, eating. I take a few bites, thinking there's something pathetic in his close attention to his eggs.

After he rinses the dishes, he fusses with his AeroGarden on the counter, gently cutting basil, and placing the basil in a baggie.

"You like basil. These are for you," he says, a sheepish expression on his handsome face. "Anything can grow in the right light."

I glance at my watch. "So the depraved woman has to go home," I say, wanting to leave. To figure all this out.

"No. I'm the depraved man," he says darkly. Then he looks around the room. "Don't forget your basil. Do you have your earrings? Glasses?"

Later, when I'm home, I can't write. I feel empty, because this morning, everything changed again. "I love you," he said, but where is the passion of last night? Is he unable to sustain his emotions beyond the night? Is he sorry he told me he loved me? Why he was impotent?

I open the windows wide, letting in the clear, sunlit air. A yellow butterfly flutters by my windowsill, so beautiful, and for a while I watch it sputter away.

The sun is bright today, and a slow, warm wind covers the city like smoke. I close my eyes and let my mind travel to anywhere, and soon I'm riding my magic carpet, writing love scenes, using images from my dreams as background—a tree catching the light like a ball, a black swirl, the cave's sudden darkness . . .

After I have my coffee, bathe, and get ready for the day, at the computer I draft "Mr. X Is Back. Will It Work?"

I want you back. I love you, he said. *But this morning on the drive to my apartment, Mr. X was once again distant, closed up, as if the night's closeness was too much for him.*

For the next few hours, I write, lost in the world of Mr. X. I finish the draft, planning to read it later at Starbucks, then to edit it. By now, late afternoon is here, a pale sunlight competing with the push of fog.

I turn the radio to the Hispanic station, listening to Spanish music. I close my eyes, letting my mind wander. Marv and I are dancing to the sensual Spanish love song. He holds me tight, his hand firm and warm on my bare back. In my four-inch, strappy high heels, my mouth is even with his. We kiss, our bodies barely moving, and when the music stops, we are still kissing and the room is empty.

I jar myself into my reality. In a surge of energy, I paint the wall next to my bed with a mass of white roses, their green stems curling and winding along the edge of the wall. I paint for two hours. When I'm finished, I'm happy I did it. I like it.

I put on my backpack and hurry outside, into the fading light.

Chapter 25

Lisa had her hip surgery. A few days later, Janet and I visit Lisa at her home, an elegant one-story house in Pacific Heights. Local artists, including two of my lady-in-box paintings, cover the walls. The teak floors are highly polished, and antiques mix with Mies van der Rohe chairs.

Lisa, wearing a pale blue silk robe, appears frail. She sits on a wingback, beige velvet chair in her ice-blue bedroom. A walker stands next to her chair. Photographs of her son and grandson are framed and displayed on glass tables, along with photographs of the three of us.

Lisa doesn't want to talk about her health and dismisses our concerns, so we chat about my latest evening with Marv.

"Vegas now. His gem show again," I say. "So for sure he's

in Vegas with the ex-wife, the one he promised he wouldn't see anymore."

"Honey, this is not good," Janet says.

"I should never have gone back to him," I say.

"I smell a rat," Lisa says. "The dog is in the kennel because he's with her." Lisa's coral lipstick is bright against her pale face. Vials of medications are on the antique table next to her.

"He said he didn't want to be without you. But he can't give more. You're getting his best. You got Mr. X. Go with that," Janet says, applying orange lip gloss on her lips. She wears an orange sweater and black leggings and black ankle boots with zippers on their sides.

"Bull crap. He watches too many Cary Grant movies," Lisa says.

"Is good sex enough? That's where we work best—lovers in the dark—but we don't work outside of that, and unfortunately, I need more. I want something that I haven't had." I sigh. "I told you, he was impotent."

"Maybe he was nervous about his declaration that he can't live without you," Lisa says.

"Nervous my ass," Janet says. "Nervous about getting caught in a lie again. The man was impotent because he knew he was lying."

"Have you checked to see if he's on JDate?" Lisa asks.

"Yes. He hasn't been on," I say.

"Keep checking," Lisa advises.

"I doubt that he'd go on now."

"Doubt what?" Lisa says imperiously. "You're smarter than that. He's stupid. He thinks because he's an oh-so-gorgeous, wealthy male on Viagra he can get away with anything."

"I love him. Even though I know he's a no-show, I love him."

"You love Mr. X more," Lisa says.

So when I get home, first thing I check JDate, and sure enough, Marv was on JDate this morning.

Okay. This time I'm going to win. I have a plan. I log in to membership and create a new profile, calling myself Dancer Diva. I fill out the necessary stuff, then I write my profile. *I'm thirty-two years old, and an actor. I love older men. They are so much more interesting.* Then I scan and post a photograph of myself at thirty, wearing dark glasses and a polka-dot bikini, lying by my pool in Happy Valley.

I wait. An hour later, Marv e-mails Dancer Diva, *You're a gorgeous woman. I like that you're an actor. And young. I travel around the world, selling diamonds to celebrities. You look like a diamond. I'll be in Vegas for a few days, but e-mail me. Great Guy.*

I write my next Mr. X column, telling my audience about my plan, then post Marv's response to Dancer Diva. The plan is when I get enough Dancer Diva responses, I will make a time to meet and tell him I'm Dancer Diva. That will be it.

For the next twelve days, I write, sometimes three times a

THE VIAGRA DIARIES

day, ardent e-mails to Marv, signing myself Dancer Diva. He responds. I post his responses in my columns, and immediately the fan mail accelerates. The columns are going great. Local television and radio stations invite me to talk about boomer dating. A Hollywood agent contacts Monica. The agent wants to option the columns for a movie. Monica says we'll take our time. "Those Hollywood people are vultures," she says. I'm excited about my career and feel as if anything I want to do is possible.

I write "When Is It Time to End It?"

When is the time? Mr. X is deliciously guileful, his moods a variation of a boy's on the sexual prowl—high, low, hidden, never the same. There is never a good time to end it because the neurosis is always there, but as I watch Mr. X hurry to his car, my heart is beating so fast. . . .

Two days later, I'm at the computer and Marv calls. "Honey, I've missed you," he says.

"That's nice," I say.

"Do you miss me?"

"Madly."

"Then what about tonight?"

"I can't. I'm sorry. I'm really busy with my column, and then I have dinner plans."

"Tomorrorw?"

"Can't this week," I say.

"What about next Saturday night? Dinner. A weekend with me?"

"It's my birthday on Sunday so I'm tied up."

"Happy birthday. I'll take you out the following Saturday night. We'll celebrate then?"

"I'll let you know," I say.

Chapter 26

Sunday morning, the day of my birthday, I receive a bouquet of pale gold roses from Ryan, with a lovely card. *You're ageless, Anny. Always, Ryan.*

I stand in front of the mirror, noticing the loose neck, the pouch under my chin, and the faded and thinning eyebrows. I listen for the phone call that doesn't come. Of course Marv forgot my birthday, or did he?

I finish dressing. I'm meeting Emily and Harry at Golden Gate Park, then we're having dinner at Sam's, my favorite San Francisco restaurant. Before I leave, I log in to JDate and read the glowing romantic e-mails for Dancer Diva, from Marv. *We should meet soon. When are you free?*

•   •   •

take a taxi to the park and meet Harry and Emily at the entrance. Fred jumps on me and almost knocks me over, licking my face, my hands. Laughing, Emily pulls him away, telling him not to knock over "Grandma." Emily looks so pretty—violets wrapped around her ponytail and her face devoid of makeup; she has a natural beauty, the kind you notice after you know her.

"Happy birthday, Mommy," Emily says, giving me a bear hug.

"Happy birthday, Mom," Harry says with a wink. "We have your gift in the car. We'll give it to you at dinner."

It's so beautiful here, blossoms covering the lawns like pink chiffon. We lie on the grass, watching Fred romp and run to catch a ball Harry throws him, Fred's shadow floating along the grass.

I watch a ladybug crawl along a blade of grass, remembering my brother chanting, "Ladybug, ladybug, fly away home." I let the ladybug crawl along my finger, wanting to keep it, to take it home. But it's too beautiful. I shake it loose and watch it fly away, sputtering in the air, then falling to the grass.

"Mom," Emily says, "I'm glad you're with us today. This is fun."

"I love being here with you too," I say.

"Did you get dozens of roses from Mr. Wonderful?" Emily asks.

"I didn't tell him it's my birthday," I lie.

"You shouldn't have to tell him," she persists.

"I want you to meet my uncle," Harry says. "He's got a

nice house in Santa Cruz and gardens all day. He's got plenty of money too."

"She'd be taken care of for life," Emily says, looking at Harry.

"I don't want to be taken care of. I'm making money. I'll make more. Stop trying to mate me."

Emily heavily sighs, giving Harry a knowing look. "Mom, we just don't want you to be alone."

So while they rant on about the singles groups I should join, the things I should do, I close my eyes, admiring the fractions of sunlight floating in balls, then disappearing, imagining that I'm sinking into the flat, lime-green lawn, remembering Emily as a child, at her play table, carefully hammering the pegs into the holes. Her bib smelled like apricots and rubber.

"Mom, wake up. We're going," Emily calls.

The next night I'm home relaxing and watching *Cheaters*, this awful reality show about these lowlifes cruising around in a detective's van, sobbing about their mates' infidelity until they find the cheaters. I switch channels, passing *Dr. Phil* reruns and *The Bachelor*, about these dumb girls sobbing over a nebbish, recycled bachelor. When the phone rings, I'm startled. It's close to midnight, and it's Lisa.

Excitedly, she tells me that she went to a posh Jewish Federation fund-raiser with her boyfriend. "So who did I see but a tall, good-looking man wearing a name tag with the name Marv Rothstein on it. He was with a tall, anorexic-looking woman. She was very young but pretty, though. We were introduced and he pretended not to know me, which is ridiculous, because you've told him about me. Anyway, it was one of those thousand-a-plate dinners."

I hold the phone tight.

"Why doesn't the big man ever take you?"

"I don't care about those events," I say.

"I advise feng shui," Lisa says, lowering her voice. "It will change your life. I was in turmoil. After the feng shui guy came to my house, I sold two buildings and then I met Harold. Okay, I'm not head over heels, but he cuddles and he's consistent. Anyway, let me give you the feng shui guy's phone number. He's incredible. Very spiritual. He'll change your life."

After I hang up, I pace back and forth. I'm angry with myself for staying so long. How will I end it? I still haven't called and let him know about Saturday night. It dawns on me: I'll contact Great Guy, pretending I'm Diva Dancer, and ask to meet him tomorrow night. Then I'll tell him face-to-face that the gig is up. At last he'll know that I'm onto him.

Excited now, I log in to JDate, click on Great Guy, and write, *I'll be in San Francisco tomorrow night and I'm dying to meet you. You are so handsome, so charming. Please meet me at the top of the Mark Hopkins Hotel at seven. You'll know me. I'll be wearing a long red coat. My real name is Natasha.*

Two hours later, at 2:00 a.m., he replies, *Can't wait. I'll be sitting at the bar.*

Chapter 27

I arrive early at the Mark Hopkins Hotel in Nob Hill. The fog has settled over the city, and it's freezing. I'm wearing a long, red coat and black, platform shoes. Also, I'm wearing a red beret with a crystal butterfly clip on it.

A moon sits in the dark sky like a golden ball. Cable cars are chugging up the hills, and Grace Cathedral glows like a white dream.

I inhale the cold fog and hurry into the hotel. The grand lobby has massive, high ceilings, crystal chandeliers, and old, paneled walls. I ride the glass elevator crowded with tourists to the top of the hotel. I close my eyes and hold my breath.

The elevator doors open to a plush red and crystal large room. Tourists wait in line for a table. Standing behind the line, I watch Marv sitting at the end of the long, mirrored bar. A pianist wearing a white tuxedo is playing "It Had to Be You," and couples glide in circles on the small dance floor. Crystal chandeliers hang from the high ceiling like jewelry, and tall windows look out at stars so close they almost touch the windows.

As I watch Marv, so elegant in his dark suit, impatiently glancing at his watch, his lovely long hands nervously smoothing his perfect hair, I'm remembering the first time I saw him. I was breathless. I'm still breathless, watching him. Impervious to his vanity, narcissism, lies, I feel a sudden, overwhelming feeling of love for his wounds, his defenses, his vanity, and even his deceits. I know that if I let him know that I'm Natasha, I'll humiliate him forever. Make myself look absurd, mean, even like a stalker. At this moment I know that I've loved him, will always feel love for him. He gave me a gift, awakened my sexual passion. Each time we made love, he was like a young soldier on his way to war, and that's the way he is. He lives every moment, his way.

Yes, I'll see him Saturday night and tell him it's over. But I'll never tell him about Dancer Diva. I'll let him have that.

I hurry into the elevator and a waiting taxi.

The next morning I e-mail Marv that I'll have dinner with him next Saturday night.

Saturday night, Marv and I are at the North Beach Restaurant, having dinner. He looks tired. His usual glowing olive skin is pale and mottled. He's been talking about his "business trip," and the fabulous yellow diamond he sold to a rock star. He wants to buy a flat in London.

"Wonderful," I say.

"You look wonderful, Anny. Glowing."

I smile.

"Anny, I missed you. I miss your quirky ways, your dramas. You're beautiful. I miss your body, the way you feel," he says, lowering his voice.

"Marv, we need to talk."

He half-closes his eyes, sighs heavily, as if bracing himself for a confrontation. "I know that I don't pay enough attention to you. We're older now, Anny. It's different. At our age, what we have is special." He smiles, holds my hand. "You're still the best sex I've ever had."

"Marv, it's over. I've wanted to tell you—not to call me anymore. Please, Marv. I was weak when it came to you, but I'm in another place now."

He strokes my hand, looking at me the way a wistful boy looks at his mother. "Well, Anny. Whatever you want."

"It's not what I wanted. It has to be."

He glances at his watch. "I want to show you my new bench. My decorator bought it in Paris—"

"Marv, I'm taking a taxi home. It's over."

Slowly, as if thinking I'll change my mind, he pays the bill and then stands. As we make our way through the crowded restaurant to the front door, he stumbles.

"I got you," I say, holding his arm.

"I must have had too much to drink." He looks embarrassed.

"Let's get some water," I say, but it's too late. He collapses. He's lying on the floor, his color gray and his eyes rolled back. "Help! Someone help!" I scream. "Please, quickly. Please, please!"

"I'm a doctor! Call 911!" shouts a short man with red hair. The doctor orders everyone to clear out, to give us room. He removes Marv's tie, opens his shirt, and pounds his chest. He's turning grayer. Everything is happening so fast. Medics arrive and place an oxygen mask over Marv's nose.

Outside, the medics place Marv in the ambulance and I ride in the back with him. His color is almost blue and his eyes are closed. A medic sits on each side of him, looking grave.

At Mt. Zion Hospital, they rush him down a hallway and the doors slam shut. A nurse asks if I'm a relative.

"No, a very close friend. I'd like to stay."

She takes me to the ICU waiting room and promises to let me know his condition as soon as the doctors know.

I sit on a plastic chair, drinking bitter coffee. Please don't die, I repeat to myself. I never told Marv that no matter what, I would always feel love for him—that he gave me something I hadn't had for a long time, something that I had thought was dead. His words before this happened are no longer important.

The door opens. A nurse wearing a mask around her neck comes into the room. "Are you a relative of Mr. Rothstein?"

"A friend."

She looks sympathetic. "He's had a severe heart attack. The next twenty-four hours are crucial. The doctors are working on him. Unless you're family, it's best that you go. Call the hospital tomorrow."

As I walk toward the elevator, I see a tall, blond, handsome man rush down the hall. I recognize Marv's son, Maurice, from the photo in Marv's living room. He has Marv's strong chin, long mouth, and high cheekbones. I stop him. Explain that I was with his father.

"You're Anny," he says.

I nod.

"As soon as I know anything, I'll call you, Anny."

I wait all day, and no call. Late evening, I call the hospital. The nurse tells me that Marv is in surgery. He's having a triple bypass. He'll be in ICU for several days.

"When can I see him?"

"You'll have to call his son."

Maurice's number is listed. I leave a message: "Please call."

Days pass. I say prayers for Marv's recovery. When I pray, I go to St. Marks Catholic Church in North Beach and light candles for the saints. I feel close to the Catholic Church and I feel a calling there. I love the rituals, colors, pomp, and faith. Later, when I call the hospital to inquire about Marv, a nurse says that he's in "critical condition."

I close my eyes, remembering my mother's funeral. She was cremated. The gold cardboard box with her ashes is on display. The rented rabbi screeches in a high-pitched voice about her "wonderful" life.

Rain rattles the windows.

Evening soaks the room, the sound of the rain slamming the windows strangely comforting. Marv's illness exacerbates an overwhelming compassion for him, and the thought that he might die frightens me. He has had an important place in my life.

To relax, I prepare to work on a painting. I lay out the palette, deciding to use grays and greens and whites—a touch of emerald. Just as I begin the painting, the phone rings. It's Marv's son.

"How is your dad?"

"He's out of the woods. He's in a private room now."

"I'm so glad to hear that . . . so relieved."

"Dr. Abrams says he needs several weeks of care and rest, but that he'll be good as new." Maurice hesitates. "He wants to see you. But call the hospital first to make sure."

The next morning, I call the hospital; the nurse informs me that Marv is weak and tired and that I can't stay long. "If you're here at four, before his dinner, that will be fine," she says.

By afternoon, it's raining hard and is cold. I wear my ankle-length trench coat. I put in my bag the framed photograph I took of Honey and hurry to the hospital.

At the nurses' station, I announce that I'm here to visit Marv Rothstein. I follow a nurse down the hall to a darkened room. A blooming plant of white orchids is next to his bed.

I tiptoe toward the bed. Marv is lying against several pillows, his face as white as his hair and his skin. "Hello," I whisper. A heart monitor is beeping, and squiggly green lines jump back and forth.

"Hello, my love," he whispers. Deep circles are under his eyes. Age spots sprawl along his arms, and tiny bruises are on his hand where an IV is inserted.

I kiss him lightly on the lips. They feel like paper.

"You smell good," he whispers, trying to smile.

I place the photograph of Honey on the bedside, next to photographs of his son and granddaughter.

"Thank you," he says. "I love it."

"I know you must miss Honey."

"I want you back," he whispers. "Anny, I love you."

"Marv. You'll be fine. You'll see."

Tears are in his eyes. "The doctors told me I can't take Viagra. I'm sorry. That's why—"

"Don't risk your health, Marv."

"Anny, lie next to me. Please."

I remove my boots, placing them by the foot of the bed. I lie next to him, careful not to push my body on his, to upset the tubes, to jar him. I hold his hand tight in mine, thinking that he's frail, so frail, utterly vulnerable. His arms, usually tan and smooth, are pale, and had I not noticed the age spots on his face? And the tiny lines along his mouth—so much deeper than I remembered. For a while, I lie here, not talking, holding hands, listening to the sounds of doctors paged, a nurse's fast footsteps in the hallway. Steam heat is puffing from the old radiator, and the sound of the rain on the windows is comforting.

"In case I die, Anny, I want you to know that I love you. There is no one else."

"Just sleep. I'll be back tomorrow."

The rain stops. The room is suddenly quiet. I put on my boots and then button my coat.

For a minute, I watch him. I kiss him on the forehead, then tiptoe from the room.

The next afternoon, when I arrive at the hospital, I hurry upstairs to Marv's room. I'm carrying a yellow orchid plant, but Marv isn't in his room. So I go to the nurses' station and ask about him.

"He's in ICU," a young nurse snips. "He had a Code Blue. The doctor is with him. No one can see him yet."

"Will he be all right?"

"I can't say. I'll tell the doctor that you're in the waiting room."

"Please don't forget."

"Yes, Mrs. Rothstein."

"I—" I start to correct her, then change my mind.

I sit in the reception room at the end of ICU. The small, orange room is empty. The air smells like bitter coffee. A television is on low, to CNN.

A striking, tall, thin, much younger woman, with unfriendly smoky eyes, enters the room. She sits across from me. Her straight, black hair hangs below her shoulders and she wears diamond drop earrings. I recognize her as the woman I saw in the *Gazette* with Marv. She removes her coat and I see clearly the gold watch with the tiny diamonds encrusted on the top of her wrist—the same gold watch I saw that night at Marv's house.

I feel duped. Stunned. All along he had lied. Yesterday from his hospital bed he lied. He's always lied. He's like those Japanese lacquer boxes: just when you think you've extricated the last box, another one pops out. I try not to stare, remembering all those times he made excuses, so many times that he said he was seeing his granddaughter, or his son, or had a doctor's appointment, and I feel my face burning.

A doctor enters the room. He wears his surgical greens, a mask dangling from his neck. "Mrs. Rothstein?"

The woman stands.

"Debra," the doctor says. "Mr. Rothstein is asking for you."

"Will he be all right?" she asks.

The doctor nods. "Follow me."

She disappears down the hall with the doctor.

I hurry toward the elevator, not feeling my feet, not feeling anything. I leave the orchid at the desk, with my card, and I go home.

After seeing Debra face-to-face, finally seeing the truth, seeing Marv's lie face-to-face, it was the last straw. I don't go back to the hospital. I send cards and a few times call Marv's son, who tells me that Marv is home recovering nicely.

My last column, "Mr. X Has a Heart Attack," caused more controversy. People write that I should never leave him now. Women write saying to let him hire a nurse. A Hollywood agent, Melissa Powell, continues to call Monica.

My new series on women and ageism is gaining recognition. CBS television interviews me at three thirty in the morning, by satellite, about older women and sex. I say that sex has nothing to do with age. "You can have bad sex at twenty, and great sex at a hundred."

I continue more speaking out against ageism.

Chapter 28

Tonight, I'm home doing laundry. Carrying my basket of dirty clothes, I take the elevator to the laundry room in the basement off the garage. It is a dank, small room, lit by a single bulb.

After I drop my clothes into the machine, I sit on a plastic chair, holding my cell phone and reading my new *Poets* magazine, the rickety machines clanking.

"There you are," says Ryan, carrying his laundry basket. "I've been calling you."

"I didn't know you were in the building." I hug him. I haven't seen him in several weeks since he was away on assignment.

We sit in the dull light of the room, talking above the whirring of the machines and clothes spinning inside. Ryan had a great trip and he's excited about his work. He's putting his award-winning photographs into a book. When the washer stops, I move my clothes to the dryer.

"I gave notice to the management that I'm moving permanently to Sebastopol," he says, looking at me intently.

"You're moving? You can't move. Who will I confide in?"

"What about Marv?"

"He had a heart attack—we're not seeing each other anyway. I told you."

"He'll want you more now. I hope you don't fall into it again, Anny."

"It's over."

Ryan pauses. "I've made up my mind, Anny. I'm moving permanently to my house in Sebastopol. I don't need the apartment in the city anymore. I'm traveling more."

He continues folding his laundry, his large, strong hands carefully folding a sheet.

The dryer is shaking and vibrating. When it stops, I fold my clothes and place them into my basket.

"Remember, Anny, I told you that I'm photographing the monarch butterflies for *National Geographic*. The Palace of Butterflies is a very special place. Few people know about it. It's a place of research and beauty. I'd love for you to go with me on Saturday. Afterward, we'll go to my house in Sebastopol. I'll cook dinner."

I nod. "Sounds great."

"Pick you up Saturday, at noon."

I hesitate a moment, watching the light shine on his hair,

wanting to thank him for always being there, for listening. Then I go upstairs.

Saturday afternoon, a day of more wind and cold, Ryan and I are on our way to Butterfly Park, near Stinson Beach. The sky is the color of charcoal and without sun. Small clouds dot the sky like cotton and seem not to move. On the way up, Ryan excitedly tells me about the migration of monarch butterflies, how they like cold weather. He knows a lot about butterflies—their origins, their habits. He loves photographing birds and wildlife.

Ryan's truck rattles along a narrow dirt road, past acres of roses of all sizes, shapes, and hues. He stops inside a forest-like garden. At the end of the garden stands a tall, palacelike structure with a glass dome, and high archways. You can see beyond to rolling hills and a low, blue sky. Distant bells chime.

"This place is set behind a convent," he explains with a whisper.

"It's so quiet," I say, holding his arm as we climb a narrow path.

"When we go inside, be real quiet. Don't touch the butterflies. They'll come to you."

We enter a room with churchlike ceilings and glass walls. I gasp. Thousands of butterflies with huge wings float in the air. Some stick to the walls; others perch on the ceiling, their wings fluttering. Their wings are in all colors and patterns, some like Tiffany glass. If nature made something so exquisite, organized its colors and lines so perfectly, then I do believe there's a divine power.

As I walk through the room, butterflies cover my clothes, shoes. I stretch out my arms and more fly to me. Their beauty is unsurpassable.

Ryan is on his knees, rapture on his strong, sensitive face, taking dozens of pictures. Butterflies perch on his hair, shoulders, and on top of his camera.

I'm not a religious person in that I don't believe in any organized religion. I do believe in the higher power, what's behind the universe, and at this moment I feel the faith nuns have, that children have, that love has. As I look at the butterfly still perched on my hand, admire its intricate beauty and steady gaze, I feel something in me has changed, something that I had kept tight. As if a light went off in me, in this moment I feel a sense of rapture, rapture for life's mysteries, exquisite moments, a feeling of freedom.

When we leave, the day is turning gray and all the light that was in the sky has disappeared into a haze of early twilight. We drive to Sebastopol. It's been a wonderful day, but as we approach the house, I feel anxiety and wonder if this was such a good idea. Only the sound of the tires on gravel invade our quiet, the kind of quiet that endures after sharing a sudden sunset, or rain, or the quick settling of night; a transformation of some kind. Never will I forget the feel of the butterflies on my skin, the look in their tiny eyes, the sudden lift of their magnificent wings. We shared something beautiful, something embedded in the mysteries of nature.

Ryan stops the truck by a tall gate, opens the gate, and then we drive up another road and finally stop in front of a small, white wood house. It's set on an acre of grass with umbrella trees, honeysuckle, and roses. The wind is up, and the trees sway. It's peaceful here. Everything, the flowers, the trees, are so cared for. Standing here in the middle of the grass and the wind, I feel Ryan's spirit.

"Anny, it's cold. Let's go inside."

Inside, Ryan's low wood house looks lived-in, with comfortable wood chairs and soft, colorful sofas that he bought at the flea markets and refinished. By a tall stone fireplace fresh logs fill a wide wicker basket, next to baskets of acorns, dried leaves, and unusual rocks he has collected on the beach. I see his curious, artist's soul in these simple objects collected from nature. Everything feels alive; open books rest on chairs and tables, and artifacts from Ryan's travels enhance the simple rooms. Photographs he's taken of artists he's met around the world hang on the walls.

"You could bring your laptop and write here," he says, dropping logs into the tall fireplace. "Or draw. It's peaceful here."

"I hope to buy a place by the sea someday. A place of my own."

"Then you will."

We sit on the lawn outside drinking coffee, eating French

bread and cheese Ryan bought at a country cheese shop on the way up, talking. We talk about everything from Latin music we both love to the recent gallery openings in the city, sometimes both talking at once. Ryan holds his Nikon; every so often, when I'm not aware of it, he clicks a picture of me. He talks about Ireland—"the beauty of the grasses, the castles, the people. It's like no other, Anny."

"I'd love to see where James Joyce wrote his books."

"Come with me, then. I'm leaving in the spring. We'll stay in an old castle by the sea."

I sip my coffee, admiring the array of clouds turning darker and slightly moving.

"Be with someone who wants to spend time with you."

"Oh, Ryan, I—"

"I'm not asking you to marry me. We'll work, do our art, and inspire each other."

For a while, we're quiet. I watch a squirrel rush up a tree.

I say, " 'You must be able to walk firmly on the ground before you start walking a tightrope.' Matisse said that. At sixty-six I'm just getting my feet solid on the ground."

"Age has no number, Anny. You are who you are at different times of your life."

"You're only fifty-five. It's easy for you to say."

He smiles, catches a ladybug on his finger. "Look, Anny. It's good luck."

I watch it walk along his finger, onto my hand. For a while, I hold it in the palm of my hand, thinking that it's so beautiful, so perfectly designed. After a while, I watch it walk faster, try to find its way out, and I let it go to the grass again.

"Now let me take some photographs of you. Don't fuss with your hair or face; I like it the way it is—natural, funny—that's right, smile."

I'm laughing now, and soon the day fades into evening.

Later that night, I sit in the kitchen with Ryan, at a long table he made from redwood trees. Miles Davis music plays in the background. Ryan knows that we both love jazz. At his long restaurant stove, he is cooking pasta with shrimp, and chopping tomatoes for a sauce. As he works, he tells stories from his early life. He grew up on a potato farm in Ireland. At twelve years old, he came to the United States and resided with his parents in Los Angeles. He worked himself through UCLA, studying landscape architecture and then photography. Later on, he did his graduate work at the Chicago Art Institute.

"You never talk about your wife," I say, aware that he seems suddenly moody.

"Sarah was great," he shrugs, sadness in his eyes. "Let's talk about this wonderful day, being together."

"Ryan, do you think the past makes us who we are? Can we develop into new people, or do we always make the same mistakes?"

He shrugs. "I think the past is a wonderful reference. Our lives are like a movie. We can watch it, see what works, what doesn't. Anyway, Anny, let's have dinner."

After we eat our dinner in the large, warm kitchen, we sit on cushions by the fireplace, drinking hot brandy. Ryan puts on Gypsy music, and for a while we're quiet, just enjoying the sensual music.

"I'll never forget the look on your face when you were with the butterflies," Ryan says, tenderly sweeping away a strand of hair from my eye.

The wind rattles the windows, and the sound of thunder echoes in the distance. "It's beautiful here," I say, leaning on his shoulder.

"You're beautiful," he whispers.

He takes me into his arms and kisses me. At first, I pull back, hesitate, but he's persistent, and then I kiss him back, and the kiss is long and tender, and soon, like lustful teenagers, we're kissing like wild. Until I pull away. "I shouldn't . . . we shouldn't—"

"It's too late, Anny. We have to."

The kissing is more urgent. I'm feeling aroused, enjoying his passion, the way he makes me feel. Ryan kisses slowly, tenderly, quietly, gently touching me the way I'd seen him touch the roses, or the butterflies.

He takes my hand then, and willingly I follow him into his bedroom.

•   •   •

The room is dark except for a moonbeam that throws a light across the simple double bed. Not feeling self-conscious, but empowered and sexually alive, I get into bed. Ryan's body is firm and youthful. For a while, we lie still, the moonlight casting our naked bodies into silhouettes. So beautiful, I think. It's quiet, except for the wind's rustling. I feel suddenly self-conscious, that tentative feeling you get as a child when you go to a forbidden place.

We make love then, silently, and tenderly, and it's wonderful. When it's over, we lie in each other's arms.

"Too bad we don't smoke," I say, trying to break the sudden tension. "This is a time when lighting cigarettes would fill in our quiet."

"Anny, tonight was wonderful."

"Yes, it was."

He kisses me for a long time. Then we settle into sleeping positions. He holds me tight. Soon he's asleep, slightly snoring. I can't sleep. I feel uncomfortable, out of sorts, the way one feels when dislocated. Suddenly I feel sad. I remember how it felt with Marv holding me during our sleep, how he smelled and slept silently like a child sleeps without a sound. Gently I unclasp Ryan's arms from around my waist and move to the side. I lie awake until dawn spreads along the room, wanting to go home.

•   •   •

The next morning when I awake, sunlight pours into the room. Ryan is downstairs, making breakfast. I stretch my arms, feeling slightly panicked, and wanting to go home as soon as possible. In the light of day I know that I did the wrong thing. I'm not ready to be with anyone, and I don't want to lead Ryan on. Nor do I feel that passion I had felt with Marv. All those times Marv was in a hurry to take me home, he probably felt what I'm feeling this morning.

Quickly, I bathe and dress and go downstairs. Ryan, shirtless, wearing jeans, is making omelets and coffee. He hugs me. "Morning, darling. Hungry for breakfast? I cut some lavender roses for you. Remember, Anny, cut the stems underwater before you put them into the vase."

"Thank you, they're beautiful."

At breakfast we talk about his gardens and plans to renovate the house. "I could build you a studio by the roses. Isn't it perfect, Anny? A perfect place for you to paint."

"I plan on buying my own country place."

"I have some photographs to show you." He opens a tall envelope and gently lays along the table black-and-white photos of hawks in motion. The way he photographed them is so unusual, as if they're blurred, their huge wings caught inside moving clouds.

"I never knew hawks were so beautiful," I say, admiring the photos. "They're majestic."

"Hawks have the ability to hang motionless in the air," he says, a light in his eyes. "They ride strong winds."

He replaces the photographs in the envelope. "I'm having an exhibit of the hawks at a new gallery in New York."

I continue eating in silence.

"Stay with me this weekend."

"Don't, Ryan. I loved last night. But it's not what you think."

"Is it Marv?" he asks after a long silence.

"No." He looks at me, hurt in his eyes. "I feel terrible. I really like you. I don't want more, Ryan. I can't."

He looks perplexed. He gets up and rinses the dishes. "I thought we'd explore the village today."

"Ryan, don't. We're not that couple. We can't be that couple. I'm sorry."

"But last night—"

"Forget last night. It should not have happened," I say, surprised by my harsh words.

"I see." He looks so hurt.

"You don't see. I see that I'm not ready to be with anyone right now. I have my career—I need time to work on myself, on my relationship with Emily. I didn't mean to hurt you."

He presses the edge of the envelope with the photographs, his artistic fingers smoothing the creases flat. I feel bad. I know I've hurt him, and I know what that feels like. I also know that I need time to resolve Marv.

Ryan stands. "Anny, I don't want to see you for a while. I trusted you. And you broke my heart. I'll take you home now."

Chapter 29

"I studied the slides you e-mailed," my dealer, Inga, says on the phone. "I love them. I'm offering you a solo show in February. Are you ready?"

"Am I ever! I'm thrilled, thank you. I've been working three years on this group of paintings and boxes."

"I love the paintings of the women in hats. They have a line like de Kooning."

"Wow."

She tells me she will work on the invitations and asks me to send her a mailing list. Her art truck will pack the paintings and bring them to the gallery.

After I hang up, I sit a while by the window. I feel triumphant. I think about all the years I fantasized about having a solo exhibit. Yes, anything is possible. At any age you just have to believe in yourself and work hard.

The holidays approach. I have a small tree on my glass table. I decorated it with strands of plastic pearls and silver bells. A silver star shines on the top. I haven't heard from Ryan since that night in Sebastopol. I feel sad about this and wish him the best. At times, I miss him terribly.

On Christmas Day, I take the BART train to Berkeley. Emily and Harry are having some of their relatives, friends, and neighbors to a Christmas party. The train is swaying and I'm holding the spinach-noodle cheese-casserole I made and a bag of gifts. When the train goes through the tunnel, I hold my breath, praying the train won't get stuck under the water. A heavy man sitting next to me is ranting about the last time the train got stuck and people were trapped for hours. He has long, thin hair and foul breath.

At the Berkeley station, I rush down the long flight of stairs to the front entrance, where Harry and Fred are waiting in Harry's SUV. Harry is wearing a Santa Claus sweater, his black hair puffed high.

"Grandma is here," I say, getting into the car and kissing Fred.

Driving into traffic, Harry tells me about the feast Emily has spent days baking and cooking.

"She's amazing," I say, Fred licking the top of the casserole.

"She worries about you," he says in a confidential tone. "We like Ryan."

"So do I. Ryan and I are friends," I say in a singsong voice.

"No offense, Anny, but you told Emily that you stayed the night in Sebastopol."

"That doesn't mean—"

"It does to her!" he shouts. "Don't tell her so much. We worry."

"Not to worry. I'm fine. I'm happy. Doing well."

"Maybe you should go on eHarmony. I see those television ads of seniors falling in love. They look so happy."

"They look lobotomized," I snap. "Love is not a résumé. It's something that happens."

Finally, we arrive at Emily and Harry's beautiful house, which Harry designed. It's steel and glass with thirty-foot ceilings, concrete floors, and built-in bookcases that go all the way up to the second story. Set in the middle of a courtyard surrounded by Japanese maples, it has the feeling of a small glass church.

Emily, wearing a red tunic over a leotard, and red, open high heels, gives me a huge hug. I follow her to the open kitchen.

"The casserole looks great, Mom," she says, taking it from me. A huge turkey is cooling on a platter on top of a white, long marble counter, along with various platters of pâtés, hams, cheeses, and salads. Everything is organized, beautiful, and perfect. The long glass dining table is set with a gold cloth. White roses fill rows of square glass vases, and sprayed-gold pinecones decorate the center of the table.

"Mom, play with Fred. Make sure he has his binky. He gets crazy if he doesn't have it. It's the yellow duck. And be careful on the stairs. All we need is for you to fall. Harry says you don't look where you're going."

"All we need is for you to fall," Harry repeats. He's at the bar, arranging the bottles of liquor.

"Harry, she can't see well!" Emily shouts.

While Emily finishes arranging the table, I sit on the floor with Fred, playing go-get-the-binky until the guests arrive. The relatives and neighbors and friends bring gifts, and Harry makes drinks. My aunt Zoë, who is eighty and wears a rhinestone tiara on her teased, tan hair, is drinking vodka and getting "tipsy," as she says. Everyone is drinking, munching on crab cakes and dip. Christmas music is blasting, and I'm dancing the twist to "Jingle Bells" with this neighbor Andy, who wears a huge Mohawk and a Rolling Stones T-shirt. Other neighbors, contractors who work for Harry, who have brought gifts and platters, also start dancing.

"Oh, my God, my turkey!" Emily shrieks. "Fred is eating the turkey!"

Poor Fred is under the table gobbling the turkey, and Emily is sobbing that her dinner is ruined. Harry grabs the turkey from Fred, and I'm assuring Emily that I hate turkey and, anyway, she has too much food. "No one will care," I emphasize.

"Bad boy!" shouts Harry to Fred. In a stern, fatherly voice, he lectures the poor dog that the turkey "cost a fortune," and that now they don't have a turkey.

Finally, dinner is ready. Everyone is gorging on casseroles and home-baked pies.

"What are you, a bunch of goyim?" shouts Aunt Zoë. "Lights, trees, hams? Oy."

"Mother, please," warns her daughter, my cousin Marcia.

"We love Christmas," I say. "I'm more interested in Christmas than Judaism."

"Goyim," Aunt Zoë mutters, stuffing her mouth with pumpkin pie.

"Gift time!" Emily calls into a megaphone. Emily is calling out the names that are in a hat, and everyone is tearing open gifts and talking over each other while Fred tears up the paper. I notice that some of the gifts are recycled from last year. I open three jars of year-old jam, a hideous knit scarf from a cousin, and an even uglier sweater with a fake fur collar from my cousin Boo Boo. I get a microwave and a subscription to AARP from Emily and Harry. I try to act excited.

"Now you can live like a person. Stop heating stuff on the stove like the homeless do," Emily advises.

"Stop heating your food in the oven," Harry says, a sympathetic look on his face.

"You can bake potatoes in it," Emily says.

Then the night is over. The relatives, neighbors, and friends stand in line and Emily fills their Tupperware containers with leftover food. Fred scarfs down part of a casserole he dragged under the table.

After Emily and I clean up the kitchen, I go to the guest

room, where I change into my new red flannel pajamas, then slide into the Japanese-style bed, which is so flat on the ground I have to bend real low to get in it. Fred is lying beside me, his binky under his paw.

"I brought you a fan," Emily says, coming into the room. "I know you can't sleep without one." She's wearing the big, red, fuzzy robe I gave her. Her black, silky hair hangs loose to her waist. She places the fan on the nightstand next to me and plugs it in.

"Great. Now I can sleep," I say.

"And Harry schlepped to Longs and bought your favorite cherry cough drops. They're in the drawer next to the bed."

"How nice."

She watches me a moment. "Mom, Ryan loves you, and he's a wonderful, interesting man. Get married before it's too late. Marv only said he loved you because he's kicking the bucket and can't take Viagra."

"I don't see Marv. Leave him alone. Besides, I don't want to marry again."

"Why not?!" she shouts, her face turning red. "Do you prefer staying in your studio writing and talking on the phone all night with your deadbeat girlfriends? You need to talk to your therapist about this."

"You're not married," I dare to say.

"But you're old, Mom. I don't want you to be alone."

She stands next to the bed, watching me as if waiting for some revelation, for something to change. I bite my tongue, not daring to tell her that she's the one who should be married and what is she waiting for? Then she kisses me good night, smooths the blanket over me. "Night, Mom. I love you."

"I love you too."

"Harry will drive you home tomorrow. We don't want you taking BART. You don't see well and you could fall. All you need is a broken hip."

We kiss good night one more time, then she goes upstairs.

For a while, I listen to Fred's snoring, feeling fortunate that I have Emily, Harry, Fred, my life.

Chapter 30

I'm home writing "Age Rage," a piece about society's anger at age. I'm deep in thought when I hear the phone ring, but I can't find it anywhere. It rings persistently, and I run around looking for it. It's not in the closet or in my jacket pocket or under the couch. Where did I put it? Am I forgetting things more than usual? Keys? Leaving my bank card in the ATM and forgetting my PIN?

I follow the faint beep. It's near my bed, not under it. I pat down the bedspread like patting down a criminal. Got it! "Hello."

"Mom?"

"Why are you crying? My God, what's wrong?"

"I'm engaged!"

I gasp. In detail, Emily relates how she and Harry had gone to celebrate their sixth anniversary at Trader Vic's in

Emeryville. When she opened her fortune cookie, it said, "Will you marry me?"

"How romantic," I gush, feeling suddenly choked up.

"Harry had the fortune cookies made. People in the restaurant applauded and shouted congratulations. Okay, Mom, stop crying. Harry says you're too emotional."

"I can't help it. I'm so happy."

"We want a small wedding, just the immediate family— maybe at Lake Tahoe, so we can bring Fred. We're going to marry on Valentine's Day."

"Sounds good." I'm relieved that they don't want a big wedding.

She pauses. "Mom, are you in the bathtub?"

"No!"

"Harry says you have a bad habit of talking on your cell phone in the bathtub. His ninety-year-old aunt Rose was electrocuted. Burned to nothing."

"Emily," I gasp.

"Mom, I have calls to make. I'll call you later. I'm so happy, Mom. I want you with me all the way."

Three weeks later, Emily and I are at David's Bridal to shop for a wedding gown. Emily stands on a wood platform in front of three-way mirrors, trying on gowns. Since Harry's proposal, Emily and I have been spending more time together than ever. We've spent hours choosing flowers for the tables, thank-you notes, wedding guest books for the guests to sign, then finally, at Noah's in Berkeley, choosing the salads, bagels, and smoked salmon for the wedding brunch the next day. I've spent hours with Emily and Harry registering at Macy's for dishes and silver, and it's so much fun. Perfectionists, Harry and Emily fussed for hours whether they wanted square dishes or round, carefully choosing what color sheets they wanted, what size towels.

I'm feeling all teary, sitting with three of Emily's girl-friends, all of us oohing and aahing with each gown. And I'm remembering myself at Saks, choosing the gown for my wedding, trying on the Audrey Hepburn–style, silk, taffeta gown, dreaming of ending my virginity. Mother happily bragging to the saleswoman that I was marrying a "catch." I loved pleasing Mother, spending long hours with her, trying on dresses for what she called my "trousseau." To her, marriage was everything—a woman's role. A woman's "station in life," she'd say.

"Hello, are you home?" Emily snaps her fingers. "Mom, I think this is the dress. What do you think?"

"I think it's elegant." The ivory, silk-satin, strapless gown accentuates her tall, curvaceous figure, and it ripples when she walks.

"It makes me look heavy," she says, turning to the side. "I've been gaining weight."

I start to tear up.

"Oh, Mom!" She laughs. "Stop! It doesn't look that bad, does it?"

"You look like a princess."

We spend hours that afternoon shopping for my mother-of-the-bride dress. Not having a lot of money to spend, I try on dozens of dresses, but so far, I find nothing I like. Finally, we go to Loehmann's.

The three-tier store is huge, with racks of clothes from most every known designer. One floor is just for shoes and purses. It's been so long since I've shopped, but I feel really excited. Emily and I are pulling dresses off the racks, then hurrying into the communal dressing room, hanging our finds on hooks. The room, full of half-naked women trying on clothes, reeks of perspiration and cheap perfume. I try on several dresses until I find the one I want to wear—a short, simple, chiffon, black dress with long sleeves and a low, square neck.

"Perfect with Nana's pearl necklace," I say, turning in front of the mirror along the wall.

"You look hot, Mom," Emily says, looking pleased. She smiles. "I like it."

"Good price."

We go to lunch at Mama's, Emily's favorite place. We eat Slim Joes and drink Diet Cokes. Then I can't help it; I ask if she and Harry are going to have children. "Not that I'm intruding. I mean, I just wonder—"

"I'm not sure, Mom. It scares me to think of a pregnancy." Her expression changes from girlie glee to serious contemplation.

"Emily, I'm sorry I wasn't more present in your childhood. But that doesn't mean you'll be a bad parent. Forgive me. I didn't mean—"

She holds my hand, tears in her black eyes. "Mom, you didn't iron my clothes or bake cookies or make lunches—and, yes, you put my sandwiches in the freezer and then into my lunch box, and they'd be all soaked. But you dressed up as a witch on Halloween, played games with me. You taught me how to finger-paint. You were a magical mom."

We resume eating our lunch. For a minute, we don't talk. I'm feeling emotional, wishing I could go back in time and parent Emily all over again, not be that numb, angry parent ignoring this beautiful child. But Emily's devotion and love is a gift, and I don't want to spoil the day with my sudden saddened mood. So, after lunch, giddily, we proceed to the shoe store.

Chapter 31

B etween my writing, my art, and the wedding plans, I'm as busy as ever. I e-mailed Ryan that Emily and Harry are getting married. For years I had confided in him my worries that Harry wouldn't ever propose. Ryan e-mailed back that he was thrilled and was going to send them a gift and wanted their address.

In the middle of everything, Monica calls. She tells me that Melissa Powell has a producer who wants to option my Mr. X columns for a feature film. Monica has spoken with her at length.

"Just talk to her. She's going to call you. Hear her out," Monica advises me on the phone. "Who knows? A film could be great for the paper."

"All right. Why not?"

So then, a few minutes later, Melissa calls. She has a fast, New York–minute voice, with a slight Bronx accent. First, she tells me how much she loves the Mr. X columns, going on about how she has a Mr. X in her life. "Mohammed is in his late fifties, and he thinks by giving me a fake Rolex watch that he can own me. I'm onto him."

I laugh.

"Anyway, I've been stalking Monica. I love your brand on ageism; love, love, love Mr. X. I see the Mr. X columns as a movie."

I wait for her to continue.

"I have an important movie producer interested. Bruce Samson is major," she says, lowering her voice. *"Ma-jor,"* she repeats in a reverent tone. "He has the money and power to get things done. Dicks," she says, as if to no one. "They're all dicks. But he loves, loves, loves the project."

"Uh-huh. Sounds exciting."

She sighs. I hear phones ringing in the background. "However, he can't sell sixty to the studios."

"Then why does he want my project?" I ask, feeling annoyed.

"We *love* the relationship between Mr. X and the narrator. But she's sixty-five—maybe make her fifty-eight?"

"Like those drippy hair-extension housewives? No. I'm afraid that's not possible. Ageism is rampant enough in the world without turning real works into fictive dribble."

She sighs. "Well, I see your point. Hey! I'm forty-seven

and they talk retirement. But let me talk to the producer. See what I can do."

"Sure. Great."

"I'll let you know. I promise. I want this material to be in the right hands. The issues are serious."

"Wonderful, Melissa."

"The studios don't have guts. It took them decades to make *It's Complicated*. Yet even that doesn't go all the way. Mr. X is typical: slick. Terrified of age. He loves her but uses her because he thinks she's too old."

"Uh-huh," I murmur, realizing this is true. "Well, let me talk with Monica. I'd like to think about this. The real Mr. X is ill and he might be more than upset. So I'd want creative control of the project—"

"Honey, who cares?" Melissa snaps. "Would he do the same for you? Anny, the networks want twenty-year-olds. This is a long shot, so don't make it too complicated."

"I have to do it this way or no way."

"I have to bounce. But we'll talk soon. Ciao, ciao."

Later that afternoon Emily arrives with the box of acceptances to the wedding. I make apricot tea and she places on a platter, with a thin knife, a lemon cake she made fresh.

At my glass table, we sort out the *regret* and *acceptance* cards. She is glowing, her hair loose to her waist, a look in her eyes like when she'd won awards for jumping horses. Neatly, with a yellow highlighter, she marks the seating list at the restaurant. As she explains who is who on the list of Harry's relatives, I'm remembering the past weeks, planning the wedding.

Harry is paying for the wedding. It will be a simple wedding at Trader Vic's restaurant, where they got engaged. The wedding will be on the terrace, with a dinner afterward. I loved the weeks I spent shopping with Emily for a wedding cake. We'd gone to bakeries, tasting cake, until Emily finally settled on Schubert's Bakery, the oldest bakery in San Francisco and known for their real whipped crème and strawberry shortcake. We bought a fourteen-tier strawberry shortcake decorated with pink roses, Emily's favorite flower.

"So, Mom, so far one hundred and ten."

"Wow."

"All Harry's relatives are coming from New York and Jersey."

"Great."

"Of course my father sent back a *regret*." Emily bites her bottom lip. "It's probably Conchita. She's so afraid I might get ten cents."

"Emily, I know he loves you. Don't worry about that now. It's his loss."

"Mom, I arranged for Megan to do our hair at the hotel before the wedding."

"Sure. That's wonderful."

"Your hair needs a trim."

"I like it long."

We laugh then.

"Mom, I think you're gorgeous. I just want to see you—"

"Happy," I finish. "Well, I'm happy for you."

"Mom, God, it's something, isn't it?"

We hug and I hold her extratight.

Chapter 32

The morning before the wedding, Harry's family and out-of-town wedding guests arrive. We're all congregated in the lobby, kissing and whispering, "We're family now," gushing about how happy we are. Emily, looking radiant and wearing all red, shows off her diamond engagement ring, while Harry, wearing his Harvard T-shirt, shows pictures of Fred.

"He's a dog!" says Aunt Frieda in a gravelly voice. "You kids need a kid!"

"Please, God," says Aunt Zoë. She wears a pink pantsuit. Her thin, pale hair is teased high into a crown.

"Nothing wrong with a dog," says Joe, Harry's uncle.

I love Harry's parents. Lil is zippy and fun. She's petite, with thick, dark, gray-streaked hair, hazel, deep-set eyes, and a nose like Harry's. Aaron is tall, fit, and has a thick puff of black salt-and-pepper hair with a defined widow's peak and sharp, penetrating, button-brown eyes. He wears green cargo pants and white high-top tennis shoes. In a New York accent, he brags that he walks ten miles a day. He tells stories about World War II, how he was shot and saved his life by playing dead. He wears a cap with lights on it. "I can see in the dark," he says. His huge pockets are filled with trinkets he finds on the streets of New York and later sells. He's energetic and hilarious. Once he was in vaudeville. I like him.

After a while, everyone goes off to shop or do his or her thing. I spend the rest of the afternoon with Emily, picking up the wedding flowers, bouquets of pink roses, bringing them to Trader Vic's, making sure the wedding cake is delivered. At the end of the afternoon, we go back to the hotel and get ready for the evening's festivities.

The restaurant is nice. So dark you can hardly see, but it literally floats on the bay. Fishing lanterns are lit and their flames drop orange glows on the water. Fifty guests sit around a huge horseshoe table, drinking and eating steak, fish, and pasta. Everyone is giving speeches, and no one is listening. Emily and Harry, both glowing and kissing like crazy, sit at the head of the table. Aaron, wearing a dark suit, tells more war stories. Harry's cousin Seymour gives a long-winded speech about his Internet search for a woman like Emily.

"Good luck," Aunt Zoë whispers. "He fell on his head when he was ten. He's nuts."

Harry's aunt Doris has drunk much wine and is snoring loudly.

"Put a blanket over her!" Aaron yells.

"Lil said you write a column about an oversexed, seventy-year-old diamond dealer," says Blossom Cohn, Harry's cousin. She's blond, with a sharp, overly tan face, and wears a white, off-the-shoulder sweater.

She tells me that her husband, Noah—pointing to a sleazy-looking, too tan man with white hair and too white teeth—is a producer.

"Oh, great," I say.

"He's huge. Noah is the top-dog producer at Paramount. He's looking. Send me your columns. He'll get them made into a movie."

Before I can tell her thanks but no thanks, she turns her back. Aunt Belle, at 101 and still bowling, complains about her meal. "All I need is food poisoning. The last time I ate a shrimp, I landed in the hospital with tubes up my gazoo."

"Ma, eat. Don't talk," says her son, a dwarflike man hunched over his plate.

"Maury is in Chapter Eleven," says a thin woman with huge red hair. She has Parkinson's and is tied to a chair.

"What do the doctors know?" says Harry's uncle Arnold. He bends my ear, telling me that his son Louis is a genius with an IQ of 160. "He was a midget. The doctors were ready to throw him in the river. Now look. He's six feet tall."

Harry's uncle Nate raps his spoon on a glass. He stands. "We have a famous columnist in our family. Our own Anny Applebaum, the author of The Viagra Diaries."

"Oy, please, God. May she make a fortune."

They applaud.

"Viva Viagra," shouts Uncle Nate.

"They do such wonderful things these days," Aunt Zoë says.

Back in the room, I get ready for bed. For what seems hours, I lie awake. I'm too excited to sleep. Tomorrow is Valentine's Day. I can't help but look back on the past few months, waiting for Marv's pathetic calls, and plotting how to keep him. Compared to my happiness now, those short times with Marv seem so opaque, frail. I always thought that romantic love would bring me happiness. Yet at this moment—knowing that Emily is happy, that I'm doing the work I love—I feel this inner contentment, this incredible calm that I've never before felt.

I close my eyes, remembering Emily at ten. She's in gymnastics class. She does cartwheels, her long legs spinning like fans. Emily—standing on a wood stool, baking banana bread in coffee cans, planting flowers in Dixie cups. Her avocado plant growing past the windowsill . . .

Time for sleep.

It's a few minutes before the wedding. Lil and I are at Trader Vic's, waiting in the coatroom with Emily for our cue to walk to the terrace. Lil, lovely in gray chiffon and pearls, is telling Emily about the day she married Aaron, fifty-five years ago. "It's like yesterday," she wistfully says. Then Aunt Pearl, decked in red satin with a rhinestone clip in her hair, comes into the room, murmuring "Just a peek," pressing Emily close to her huge chest, telling the story about her wedding fifty years ago.

"Never go to bed angry," she advises in a raspy cigarette voice.

"Always keep him guessing," my cousin Linda advises, her large hazel eyes watering with remembrance.

"Emily's forty-two! He's fifty-one. No spring chickens!" Aunt Pearl says.

"Emily knows what to do. She loves my son," Lil snaps. A corsage of white roses from Harry is on her wrist.

Cantor Feldman knocks. "Time," he calls.

"All right, it's time. Let's go, everyone," Lil says, kissing Emily and then leaving the room.

For a moment, I look at Emily holding a bridal bouquet of white roses, a last memory before she gets married. She looks so beautiful—her ponytail held by a clip of white roses, her face glowing, and I'm feeling emotional. It's almost enough to make me forget that my new black satin three-inch high-heel shoes are killing me, not to mention my knee is acting up.

"Mom, you're crying already," Emily says, biting her lower lip.

"You look like a goddess."

"Mom, you've said that five times already."

"Well, I can't help it. You're my little girl and you look so beautiful."

"Mom, I need to tell you something. I'm pregnant."

Did I hear right? For a minute, I can't talk. It's that kind of feeling you have when you're caught totally off guard. I feel as if I were transported from the ground—up, high up.

"Mom, stop crying. Your mascara is running. Mom, you're going to be a grandmother."

"When?" I manage to say, hugging her.

"I'm five weeks pregnant. We don't want anyone to know today. They'll think we had to get married, and we didn't. We decided to get married before. So don't say anything about it."

"No wonder you're glowing."

We're hugging and I'm crying, wiping the mascara away, smoothing her dress, and then there's a knock at the door and Cantor Feldman reminds us he's ready.

Holding hands, Emily and I follow the cantor up the long, red carpet to the deck, where the guests are seated on rented chairs. The sun is setting, and the wind is up, and the ocean is roaring. Slowly, as we pass the guests, they whisper, "A beauty.

Mazel tov." Emily lets go of my hand and stands with Harry under the chuppah made of garlands of roses. I stand next to them with Aaron and Lil.

As Harry and Emily recite their vows, clusters of birds float above, as if suspended in this moment. On my other side, I hold Lil's hand. A breeze rustles Emily's train, lifting it slightly, and twilight falls on the water, gray, like silver sand.

I'm concentrating on this moment, this powerful moment of love, vowing love forever, and telling myself that I'm having a grandchild. And while they vow "till death do us part," I finally realize—understand—love binds life, is all that matters. And at this moment, standing here, witnessing my daughter's marriage, I feel whole and complete.

"I stand separate here, ready to merge my life with yours," Emily says, looking into Harry's eyes.

"I love you, but I don't own you," Harry vows. A purple satin yarmulke is perched on his head like a button.

"Our marriage will allow us to grow, to love each other every day with new understanding," Emily recites, looking adoringly at Harry.

"I pronounce you husband and wife! You may kiss the bride!" Cantor Feldman shouts. Harry and Emily kiss, and the guests shout, "Mazel tov!"

Aunt Zoë is throwing rose petals, Uncle Nate is throwing coins, and the younger kids are grabbing the coins, and then the photographer is following and taking pictures. The DJs are playing music, and the bartenders are serving drinks.

Guests are standing in line at the open food stations, filling their plates with salmon, salads, Chinese food. Everything looks beautiful—the candied hearts on every table, the fuchsia roses that Emily and I arranged inside small square vases.

I start greeting the guests; many of my friends are here.

"Honey, you look hot in that dress," Janet says. She's wearing red for Valentine's Day, her hair arranged in a French twist and sprinkled with tiny rhinestones. Her new boyfriend, Paul, dances with us. He is handsome with white, curly hair and kind blue eyes. They seem happy, and in love.

I dance with Aaron to a fast song, Aaron twirling and dipping, bragging that he used to win jitterbug contests.

I laugh. "You're funny. And a good dancer."

"Not so bad yourself," he says, spinning me around.

The music stops for a break. The guests go to the buffet and gather in groups. I sit at a table, catching my breath and taking from my evening purse my lip gloss to refresh my lips. When my cell phone rings, I think it's the lost-and-found at Trader Vic's, hoping that they found my pearl bracelet, which I had earlier discovered was missing.

"Hello, Anny; it's Marv."

I hold the phone tight. "How are you?" My heart is beating so fast.

"Never better," he says in a buoyant voice. "I wanted to call and to thank you for your get-well cards."

"I can't talk. Emily and Harry got married today. I'm busy."

"Oh, congratulations. Well, I wondered if we could have dinner or something—"

"No, I don't think so. I have to go, Marv. Good luck."

When I hang up, I feel slightly woozy, the breathless feeling I've always had when hearing his voice. But then I remind myself that it's over, and what I'm really feeling is compassion, and a sentiment that will never go away. It's amazing. Sometimes you bond with the wrong person, but the bonding remains forever. When I look back, I know he had a place in my journey to where I am now.

The night is going so fast, fast the way light turns to dark, so fast, spinning, spinning like lights spinning. A grandchild, I keep telling myself, a grandchild, and as if some awakening has happened in me, something has changed. For the first time ever, I feel as if I'm in another place, my past now in its own place. Oh, the music, the happiness of the night, and I'm dancing, dancing so fast my feet swell up and I take off my shoes, dancing the swing with Janet, then with Paul. Then the Jewish hora starts, and Emily, Harry, and I join hands with the guests, and circling the room, we dance so fast I can't breathe. The older relatives in walkers sit at tables, clapping and singing along.

When the "Hawaiian Wedding Song" plays, the dance floor clears, and Emily and Harry dance, dance close, their eyes on each other.

The music stops. The wedding cake is wheeled out, and Emily and Harry cut the strawberry shortcake, everyone shouting, "Make a wish!"

After that, everything is going fast. Harry asks me to dance one last dance. He whispers that he's going to tell his parents about the baby the next day at the brunch.

"I love you, Harry."

"I love you too."

We spin around and around, and I'm dizzy—dizzy, and happy. After a few more dances, the lights go on. It's time to go, time to put the memory into a photo album. Relatives fight over the centerpieces. The out-of-town relatives promise to see each other the next morning at the brunch, air-kissing and knocking on wood.

Emily wraps a piece of wedding cake in a paper napkin. "Here, Mom. Keep this and put it in the freezer. You'll eat it at your wedding."

By the time I get back to the room, it's past midnight. I soak my swollen feet in the bath, my mind replaying the wedding, its every detail. Beautiful moments slide away so fast, like memories finding a place in a book. Over and over, I tell myself that I'm having a grandchild, feeling joy, pure joy, thanking God that I have a second chance to help parent a child.

Chapter 33

It's the night of my opening. The gallery is packed. I'm standing to the side, drinking straight vodka, watching the crowd. Cuban music plays from speakers, pulsating and sensual. I'm wearing a black silk dress with long, tight sleeves and an oval, low-cut neck, and platform high heels with thin, rhinestone ankle straps. Also, like the woman in my painting *Woman Out of the Box*, I'm wearing a cluster of white roses wound around my loose chignon at my nape.

Emily and Harry arrive. Emily shows slightly and looks glamorous in a loose black dress and pearls. Her hair is arranged in a pretty, long ponytail held by a red crystal butterfly comb that I gave her. Harry looks great in black and holds Emily's hand tight. His thick hair is cut short now and wavy. He's high on his work. Recently a house he designed in the Berkeley hills won an award.

"Mom, your paintings are drop-dead gorgeous. Wow, Mom. And you look hot in that dress. I love your hair."

"I like *Girl with Dog*," Harry says. His hazel eyes shine. "It's Emily and Fred."

I nod. "I put a red sticker on it. It's your painting."

"Thank you. It's wonderful," Harry says.

Emily smiles. "Mom, we're proud of you." She looks at my drink. "Don't drink too much."

We hug. I watch them mingle with the crowd, thinking how thrilled I am about having a grandchild. There's so much to look forward to. I can't wait. Plus, I have many new goals to pursue. I feel joyful. Age is only who you are and living life to the fullest.

The music rises. Tall vases are filled with exotic crimson flowers that Inga provided. All at once, people are coming in droves. I'm happy to see painters and writers I went to college with. Then Janet and Paul, and Lisa and John, arrive. We hug and jump up and down.

"Honey, your work is drop-dead," Janet says. She wears a bright orange jacket with forties-style shoulder pads, a short skirt, and high heels. Her hair hangs in waves, and she wears shoulder-length, rhinestone earrings shaped like hearts. Paul graciously congratulates me.

"I'm buying *Lady in Black*," Lisa says. She wears a fabulous mauve, suede, fitted coat and very high heels. "I think your work is marvelous, Anny. I'm so proud of you. Isn't it, John?"

"Congratulations," he says. He's slight in build and wears a brown tweed jacket.

"Honey, there are some swell-looking men here tonight. Go for it," Janet asks.

"She doesn't care. She has a career," Lisa says, giving Janet a look.

"It's just around the corner, honey," Janet says, winking at me. "Go for it all, honey."

"I have it all tonight. I love you girls."

"Don't make me cry," Lisa says.

"We'll call tomorrow, honey."

The crowd grows. It's a mixture of art groupies I know, writers from various newspapers, young artists wearing Mickey Mouse T-shirts and fake furs, affluent collectors glancing at the art quickly, as if their brief glances will make art history. Then it blows my mind to see a red dot on *Natasha Is Out*, and a red dot on *Muses*, a painting of floating women.

When I look at the paintings, I see the years in each one. Another life, I think. Another mountain to climb. For the first time, I feel whole. I know who I am now. I know that there are new mountains to climb. A new journey awaits.

"Her paintings are poetic," says a small woman wearing this huge Hermès scarf draped over her narrow shoulders.

"What's with the boxes?" says another woman, standing close to *Girl in a Box*.

"Give me Cézanne's lemons," says a man next to her.

"Al! He paints oranges!"

BARBARA ROSE BROOKER

"Lemons, oranges—what's the difference?" he says with a shrug.

"Anny? Sam Stein."

I turn around and face a short man with a froglike face. "Yes, I know of you," I say. He's a well-known art collector and backer of independent art films. He is outrageously dressed in a green suit, a green hat shading his moon face and dot eyes.

"I'm interested in your paintings."

"Really?"

He nods. "I like *Girl in a Box*; also, the *Behind the Net* series. Excellent." He points to my seven-foot painting of a lady climbing from a box. "I like your boxes. They're different from anything else I've seen. These are about her soul."

"Yes, exactly."

He continues to talk about a film he's backing, based on detailed diaries of a seventeenth-century painter named April Bourgeois. "She painted ladies caught in boxes. Uncannily, your paintings fit her descriptions of her isolation, of trying to break out. She describes the emotions that I see in your work."

"Wow. That's amazing. So she was weird too," I say, laughing.

"Weird is good," he says, his long, rubberlike mouth stretching over small teeth. "Like April Bourgeois, you're able to convey in your paintings malaise, sadness, introspection." He looks morose. "Patronage sucks. If an artist is famous, the collectors will buy a handkerchief of snot. The yentas will salivate over a brick or a piece of string."

270

I stifle a laugh.

"I buy unknown artists before they're famous. Say! I know you write The Viagra Diaries. I love the irreverence. I like Mr. X. He's a scoundrel."

"Every man has some Mr. X in him."

He chuckles, a loud, barking laugh.

The gallery is crowded now. I'm feeling high on the vodka and the pulsating, hot Cuban music.

"I'll be back when the crowd isn't here. I'm going to buy your paintings for my film on April Bourgeois. I want a closer look."

"I'll look forward to hearing from you."

I'm sipping another drink. I look up and see Ryan standing near the entrance, looking around, trying to find me. I'm thrilled that he's here, but I feel a sudden pang of guilt.

He sees me and we hurry to each other. I'm stunned. Almost flustered. He looks great. He's wearing all black, and his hair is long and curly. We hug tightly. "I'm glad to see you," I say, my face close to his. "When did you get home? You're so tan," I nervously chatter.

He shrugs. "I've been home for a couple of weeks. I went to Italy. Swam in the Blue Grotto. Took some great photographs."

"Wow, the Blue Grotto. I was there when I was eighteen. The water is like blue velvet."

He looks at *The Swimmers*, a ten-foot painting behind us. The women in the painting are diving from high rocks, their pale bodies caught in the air, their hair floating behind them. "Anny, your work has grown, it's—magic. Don't stop painting. It goes with your work. Many of these paintings I saw in various stages."

"Yes, you did. Like you saw me in—stages. I feel bad about our last time—I—"

"Anny, that's the past. Today is the future." He looks intently at me, wisdom in his gaze. "The paintings complete you." He glances at his watch. "And I have to get going. Let me photograph you in front of *The Swimmers*. There. Smile, give me your beautiful smile."

The flash goes off. "I'll send it to you."

"Ryan, I— I'm happy to see you. I—"

"I'm leaving early for Ireland. I'll be home by summer. I'll be thinking of you, Anny." He kisses my hand. "Remember the little green ball in the glass box. Things change."

I watch him disappear into the crowd. I'm glad he was here, relieved that he still cares about our friendship. I know that I will see him someday again, and suddenly all my guilt at hurting him is relieved. He's a wonderful friend and I value what we had.

I get another drink, then talk to Monica, who is decked out in a purple dress. She's with this nice guy, a new editor at the paper. He's about forty, thin with a huge head of dark hair. "This is great, Anny," she says. "I want to buy *Girl in Red*."

"It's a gift," I say. "For all you've done."

She gets all teary. We hug, promising to talk soon. "I'll send in the next column tomorrow," I say, blowing a kiss.

I push through the crowd, stopping to greet people I know—the kids from Starbucks, couples who live in my building, even some of the boomer men I had once interviewed. It's fulfilling to see my life around me. Then the crowd thins, and only a few people are left. I find Inga at her desk. She tells me that Sam Stein bought three paintings and is coming back tomorrow.

"Great. I liked Sam," I say.

"*Natasha* sold." She smiles.

"Who bought it?"

Inga looks at the checks on her desk. "A Marv Rothstein."

"He was here?"

"Earlier today, around one p.m. he came in. He said he read about the opening in the *Chronicle*. He looked at your work for a long time. He's very interested in your work."

Inga turns the lights on and off, signaling that the opening is over.

I button my black velvet cape. By now it's almost midnight. Inga gives me a pile of the invitations, and the poster of *Natasha* that she had by her desk. I roll it up, sliding a rubber band over it.

Outside, the moon is white and the air is icy. I decide to walk to the end of the block and call a taxi. I cross the parking lot behind the gallery. The streetlights cast long streaks of dim light along the walk, and my high heels echo in the quiet. The sky is full of stars. I'm eager to get home and to ponder this wonderful night.

"Hello, Anny."

I turn around. Marv is standing by his car. For a moment we stare at each other. He's wearing a long, black coat, and in the dark his hair gleams silver.

"You look beautiful, Anny."

"Are you well?" I ask after a long silence. "It's been a long time."

He nods. "I sold my business. I'm not working anymore."

The streetlights cast an unflattering gray light on his handsome face, and he seems more bent, somehow older, diminishing into age, a place he doesn't want to be. A segment of his life he won't tolerate in himself or his women. "I'm glad you've recovered and are doing well," I say, my voice low.

He smiles. "Your show is amazing, Anny. I saw it earlier."

"Yes, Inga told me that you bought *Natasha*."

He blinks, as if reflecting. "I'm amazed how you pulled it together." He recalls when he saw the half-finished canvases at my apartment. "I never thought . . . I'm amazed." He pauses. "I like Mr. X. I've been reading your columns."

"But he's based on you. Don't you care?"

"He's a cool cat. He's . . . youthful." He looks at his watch. "Anny, please have a drink with me tonight. I have something to tell you. I'm leaving tomorrow for Paris and I need to talk with you."

"We've already done that."

"It's different now." He takes my hand.

"Are you going to Paris with Debra?"

"I don't see Debra anymore." He puts his coat collar up. "I want you to go with me to Paris. I'm leaving tomorrow at noon. I have a ticket waiting for you."

"I can't. I don't love you that way anymore. It's different now."

"Anny, I want to marry you."

"You couldn't commit beyond Monday night, so how can you marry me?"

"It's different now. We're in the last parts of our lives. Anny, you're sixty-six. Pushing seventy. Our lives are short. We're older people, and how long do you think a career is going to last? Don't throw love away."

"You threw it away a long time ago. I'm no longer interested in you that way. I have a career. I'm going to be a grandmother. And I have future goals and new choices. I've never been happier. Our ages have nothing to do with our future."

He pauses, as if making a decision. "We'll marry in Paris."

I look at his face half lit by a streetlight, his expression like that of a child who guessed the right answer. There is nothing more to say. I turn and walk up the street. When Marv calls my name, I don't turn around. I walk faster, the stars dropping light along the dark. The streetcars slide along the tracks on Market Street, and street musicians crouch on corners playing their instruments. Tomorrow is a new beginning. It always is. Every day is new and exciting.

I hail a taxi and get into the backseat. And as it drives up the hills, I watch a myriad of stars blinking and shining silver like a diamond pin, so beautiful. God, stars are something. And then I see a single star break away, change course, and soar up higher.

Acknowledgments

Special acknowledgments to my sons-in-law, Gary Osterman, for his consistent help and for listening, and always Henry Unger for his unconditional love. To my beloved brother Robert Rose and his wonderful nurses and staff at Golden Gate Healthcare in San Francisco, and to Richard Rose. To my niece Keran Davison. To Patty Axelrod, for her endless support, Wendy and Alan Riche, Aaron Kaplan, Patti Felker, Chris Abramson, Olga Vezeris, for her great help with foreign countries, and also Matthew Carlini for his patience, expertise, and endless help. My special thanks to Melissa Gramstad at Simon & Schuster for her great eye and ear and time in promoting this book. To Bradly Bessey, Frank Sanchez, Gabriel Bessey Sanchez. Always to David and Kathy Lerner. To Jerry Astrove, Donald Alex, Bill Bowker, Dr. Janine Canan, Phyllis Koestenbaum, Rose Wang, Dr.

ACKNOWLEDGMENTS

Bill Smith, Dr. Arlene Keller, Dr. John Chan, Dr. Sydney Williams, who helped me see, Dr. Jane Melnick, M.D. Tara Cortez, for her help and faith, my cherished friend Riki Rafner. Especially my students and friends from San Francisco State University OLLI. Alexander Ali for his help, my cousins Linda Diller, Nancy Rosenthal, Kelly Eder, Janet Sipos—and for all those friends I didn't mention but know who they are.

Special thanks to my muse, Lycia.